I0692339

THE FLYING COURTSHIP

THE FLYING COURTSHIP

By

E. J. RATH

AUTHOR OF "WHEN THE DEVIL WAS SICK,"
"SOMETHING FOR NOTHING," ETC.

NEW YORK
G. HOWARD WATT
1819 BROADWAY
1928

Copyright, 1928, by
G. HOWARD WATT

All Rights Reserved

THE FLYING COURTSHIP

THE FLYING COURTSHIP

CHAPTER I

A LOW-MURMURED conversation had been reaching my ears for several minutes before I paid the least attention to the words. Then it was the speaking of my own name which diverted my mind, and also my eyes, from the printed government report that I had been studying.

All that had gone before was as so much unrecorded sound; like, for instance, the medley of street noises, of which our ears are mechanically conscious, but to which our brain pays not the slightest heed until some unusual or discordant note is struck. I had been fully aware that persons were talking near me, but, to borrow a phrase from the vocabulary of the radio, the "wave length" of my auditory nerve was not attuned to the sound until I heard a man's voice saying:

"That's Mansfield!"

Mansfield is my name. I am not now, nor was I then, a personage of note or notoriety. Neither, I think, is my name an uncommon one; yet the mere pronouncement of it caused me to raise my eyes sharply from the document I held in my hands.

Nobody stood close to me. Perhaps a dozen persons, all told, were in Statuary Hall, most of them moving either to or from the corridor leading to the House of Representatives. Neither on my right nor my left was there anybody near enough to impress upon my ears, even though he spoke in a fairly loud tone, the word which had brought me so abruptly out of my preoccupation.

I glanced behind me. There was nobody there. A dozen feet back of me the white marble statue of Ethan Allen stood in heroic mold. At his left, as if to emphasize the all-inclusive scope of our national character, was the stone effigy of Calhoun, grave, stern, thoughtful. Between myself and the line of cold images of which these two formed the center, there was not a single living being.

And then I glanced down at my feet and understood. I was standing on one of the "whispering stones" of Statuary Hall. Often I had watched some venerable Capitol guide huddle his charges into a small group on one side of the circular hall, step over to the very spot where I now stood, bow his head, and mumble unintelligible things—always unintelligible to me, yet apparently wholly satisfying to his patrons. So I looked across toward the spot where I had seen the guides station their customers.

Thirty or forty feet from me stood a man and woman, talking earnestly. The profiles of their faces were close together, he looking down upon her, although she was by no means short in stature. The very height of his figure would have served to arrest my attention. There was no undue bulk in it, but evident power. As he spoke he was forced to bend his shoulders in order to bring his head close to that of his companion.

I saw a rather sharply cut face, dominated by a long, aquiline nose. He was about forty years old, I judged, and bore himself like a man in the physical condition which comes from clean living in the open.

As I watched him for a few seconds, he turned a quick glance in my direction. I did not make the mistake of dropping my eyes abruptly to the pamphlet I had been reading, like a guilty eavesdropper. Instead, for an instant I met his gaze casually; then I slowly let my glance rove to a little knot of visitors who had just come in from the Rotunda; and finally I came back to the government report.

But I was not reading; instead I was listening intently. No man, I take it, is guilty of eavesdropping when he hears his name spoken in compelling fashion by one stranger to another. Guilty or not, I was curious.

He was speaking again, but I caught only part of it.

"And he's your man."

"But, I tell you, I cannot!"

The woman's voice was low-pitched, yet it came clearly to my ears through one of the mysterious acoustic channels of the hall.

"You can—and must!"

Pretending to read and not raising my eyes, I could

nevertheless see he was looking at me as he spoke; even indicating me with a slight gesture. Clearly the name "Mansfield" had been no coincidence; I was the subject of a conversation between two strangers, and I was somebody's "man."

Dissimulation has never been in my line, but at that moment I summoned every power I possessed to make me appear unconscious of their words. Slowly I turned a page and began an apparent study of the next.

She said something I could not distinguish at all. Evidently it was in the nature of a protest, for his next words were slightly louder:

"It's your business to find out where it is. I've got to know—quickly!"

"I don't even know him," she faltered. "And I don't see why it's my business."

I could hear him laugh.

"It's easy enough to know him—for you," he answered. "He won't prove difficult. What are your looks for?"

I had paid little or no attention to the woman in my brief survey of the pair. The blunt brutality of his remark piqued my curiosity, yet I dared not look up. I heard her, however, utter an angry exclamation, which he echoed with another laugh.

"Listen!" I heard him commanding. "You can do it, and you've got to do it. It's your part of the job. You locate it, and I'll attend to the rest."

Again her voice dropped too low for me to catch the words.

"Follow him," he was saying. "Speak to him. Make his acquaintance. I don't care how you do it. Get results; that's all I'm after. And let me know to-night."

"I—I don't like it," she said. "Get somebody else, if it's got to be done."

"No; there'll be nobody else. You're the one."

"But you're sure—"

"Certainly. He's been pointed out. I watched him a good part of yesterday myself."

Here was news! I had been watched the day before, by a person whose very physique was calculated to attract even an idler's attention. It was not very flattering to my sense of observation, or else the man himself was an exceedingly clever and unobtrusive sleuth.

"If you would only—"

He interrupted her hesitating words angrily, his voice rising slightly.

"You've got your orders. Now, go to it! And remember, I want to hear to-night. Work it any way you choose, but don't fail; and don't pretend you don't know who I mean. He's the man with the pearl gray hat and the ebony cane."

Pearl gray hat and ebony cane! I was identified now beyond dispute. It had never occurred to me when I purchased that hat and stick that they were particularly conspicuous; but evidently some person thought otherwise.

With that parting description of me, he turned from

her and disappeared through the short corridor that leads to the Rotunda. Glancing warily up from my pretended reading, I saw his tall figure swing out of sight. Then I ventured a look at the woman, but she had turned toward me, and was evidently studying me. I resumed my perusal of a page on which I read not a single word.

Here was a woman set to the task of following me, of making my acquaintance, of finding out something that I apparently knew. What? And why? Certainly it was not unpardonable of me to be curious. I was amazingly so.

And why a woman? Why a woman detective? She was a detective, of course; but why couldn't a man serve? I wondered vaguely if I looked impressionable. A reluctant woman, too, which clashed strangely with my conception of the detective profession!

I stood on the whispering stone for several minutes, waiting to see what she would do. She also remained standing where the tall man had left her.

The situation was quite new to me. I was consumed with a desire to learn the outcome of it, but did not know just what I was expected to do under the circumstances. Was it my first move, or hers? How did she propose to go about the business? I was utterly ignorant of the ways of a profession that is popularly supposed to be mysterious, and doubtless is so to most people.

Patiently I remained in my place, watching her furtively, just raising my eyes sufficiently from time to time to make sure that she was there, yet at no instant getting a full or satisfying glimpse of her. I merely noted a rather tall and slender figure, clad in browns.

Inaction became tiresome after a while; it was apparent I was expected to do something. How could I be pursued, trailed, watched, have my footsteps dogged, if I did not first take the initiative of flight? Evidently mine was the first move, so I made it.

With studied unconcern—I tried not to make the act too elaborate—I first looked at my watch. It was two o'clock in the afternoon. For a quarter of an hour I had been waiting to keep an appointment with a member of the Naval Affairs Committee, and I was clearly under no obligation to prolong my vigil. Even had I felt any such obligation, I should have dismissed it as a triviality. The new situation had completely absorbed me.

Thrusting into my pocket the document I had been pretending to read, I turned slowly on my heel, without so much as a glance at the woman, and strolled off in the direction of the House of Representatives. Passing into the short corridor that leads to the main entrance of the chamber, I stepped over into one of the deep window embrasures opposite the telegraph-booths, and leaned negligently against the wall.

She was not many feet behind me. Our eyes met for an instant as she sighted me; then she passed on slowly, and paused near a group of men who were waiting at the House entrance to see various members.

Thus I obtained my first fair look at my lady of the pursuit.

It confirmed my previous impression that her height was above the feminine average. She stood very straight and slender in her knee-length pleated skirt of brown stuff and short mink coat, topped by a tiny close-fitting hat of creamy tan, trimmed with a small brown bird breast, and from beneath which showed some of the smooth dark curls of a smartly perfect, permanently-waved bob. The mottled brown and tan handbag she carried and her trim sandals, worn with creamy-tan stockings, might have come from the same lizard. I am a stickler for details, and her clever ensemble pleased my sense of the artistic. She was young, too—not more than twenty-two, I judged.

Also—and it may as well be said now, for it is the truth—she was uncommonly pretty. I cannot say she was beautiful, for to my mind that is an adjective which implies at least an approximate adherence to certain classic standards. She was not classic, either in face or figure.

There was something of distinction in her manner, however, that did not comport at all with the nature of her mission. Perhaps it was a faint suggestion of aristocracy. I was not at all displeased with my survey of her; if I had to be trailed, it was better, perhaps, to have a pursuer of decided attractions, rather than one of vulgar mold.

She stood watching me out of the corner of her eye, the brown-suède-gloved fingers of one hand absent-mindedly tapping on her lizard-skin bag. I was beginning to enjoy the situation. Evidently, though, it was not to her liking, for she seemed restless and undecided, rather curiously bereft of purpose or method for a woman who had a definite task. I could only conclude she was trying to hit upon a plan for handling her "subject"—for that, I believe, is the proper technical term for a sleuth's prey.

Her apparent reluctance to approach the issue puzzled me. It was easy for her to speak to me, if she wished. People talk to strangers every day in the Capitol. She could ask me how to find a certain member of the House, which way it was to the Senate, whether I could tell her if the Supreme Court was in session—in fact, there were a hundred casual inquiries which a woman might make with perfect propriety, even of a stranger.

Occasionally she tapped a lizard-skin sandal on the floor as if impatient at my conduct. Perhaps I was not playing the game according to regulations.

I tried another move. Swinging my cane jauntily, I stepped out into the corridor and approached her at a leisurely walk. Apparently she thought I was about to speak to her, for I was gazing at her steadily as I neared her, and she drew back against the wall with an instinctive movement.

Without pausing, I passed within a yard of her, turned off to the right, and went down the corridor leading to the west side of the House chamber. At the marble staircase I paused, to make sure she was following me, then ascended to the gallery floor and leaned over the railing to study the mammoth painting "Westward Ho!" She sighted me as she came up the stairs, and stopped on the landing, pretending to be interested in some detail of the picture.

I resumed my walk again, not hurrying, for I did not wish to put a woman to the inconvenience of haste. Crossing over to the east side of the House, I descended to the main floor and strolled back toward the Statuary Hall. She was never far behind me. I loitered in the chamber of the marble figures, and passed on into the Rotunda.

Just to the right of the entrance, as you approach the Rotunda from the south end of the Capitol, is an historical painting that always interested me, not from the standpoint of art, but because one of the Indians in the foreground is represented with six toes on one foot. I stopped for a glance at my six-toed friend, and this forced her to pass me, for she could not well loiter in the narrow doorway.

She took up a position on the other side of the big circular space, and I could observe her at some distance, without appearing to stare at her. Her indecision was becoming more and more of an enigma to me. If her duty had been merely to follow me and obtain a record of my movements, I could easily have understood her conduct; but her instructions, which I had plainly heard, were to "make his acquaintance" and to find out "where it is."

As yet she had not taken the least step toward performing this part of her assignment. True, she had received her orders reluctantly, but a detective was a detective, even if a woman, and that she had accepted the task was evidenced by her painstaking pursuit.

I started across the Rotunda in the direction of the Senate, and was halted under the big dome by a committee clerk, a friend of mine. We talked for a few minutes, the woman in brown meanwhile pacing back and forth along the wall, watching me warily, and yet apparently endeavoring to make herself think I was oblivious of her scrutiny.

I chose a time to leave my friend so that the steady pacing of her beat would bring her close to me as I resumed my stroll toward the Senate wing. We were within a few feet of each other as I passed out of the Rotunda, and there was that in her manner which led me to believe she was about to speak to me; but if she had decided to do so, her mind changed swiftly, for she let me go by unmolested.

The Supreme Court was in session, and I stepped into the solemn chamber, watching the black-gowned judges occasionally, but most of the time keeping an eye on the entrance. My pursuer did not follow. I began to wonder if she had abandoned the chase. In fact, I was startled at the thought. My own curiosity was at too high a pitch by this time to welcome such a termination of the incident. With more haste than dignity I quitted the presence of the nation's Solons.

But, no; she was still faithful to her task. I passed her again as I made my way into the Senate corridor, and once more I thought she would come to the real matter in hand. Certainly I gave her every opportunity, for I moved slowly and aimlessly, and surveyed her with a friendly and appraising glance which, I judged, ought to be sufficient to afford her an opening. She took no advantage of it; rather, on the contrary, she seemed to shrink from me.

Wondering, I kept on my way. The more I thought of the business, the more it bothered me. Without doubt it would be easy for me to throw her off my track; but I wanted to know why I was an object of pursuit, and who was pursuing me. Such a curious sort of pursuit, too! Why in the world didn't she go at her job in a workmanlike manner?

I am not a difficult person to approach; there is nothing forbidding or sinister in my appearance, so far as I am aware. She had a thousand pretenses at her command; yet she made use of none of them. Persistent in pursuit, she never made an attempt to bring the quarry to bay. It was getting too ridiculous, I thought, to last much longer; yet it did. Sometimes I feel ashamed of the manner in which I led that lady of the mink coat such a purposeless chase that early spring afternoon. Descending to the lower floor, I retraced my steps the length of the Capitol, halting in the crypt. The crypt, dimly lighted and always cold, is commonly a lonely spot, and it was so this day. She seemed baffled and timid there, but made a brave show of studying the labels on some big bundles of Con-

gressional documents that were awaiting shipment.
Of course, she knew that I knew she followed me.
I imagined this fact alone must cause chagrin to any
detective, however much of a novice he or she might
be. On the other hand, I could not help wondering
if the woman might be a consummate actress, playing
her part deliberately in this enigmatic fashion with a
definite purpose in view.

I led her through the subway to the House office-
building, around the marble corridors of that spacious
monument to the luxurious tendencies of our national
lawmakers, and back across the Capitol grounds to the
first scene of our encounter. She followed patiently
and doggedly, never approaching me nearer than was
necessary to keep me in sight. I had adopted a different manner; I feigned to be utterly unconscious
of her presence. Even when circumstances placed us
close, I gave her not so much as a glance; but always,
out of the tail of my eye, I could tell that she was still
trailing me.

It was on the broad portico that skirts the west front
of the Capitol that I saw the man again. He was talking to a companion who seemed, by comparison with
his great height, almost a pygmy. I avoided looking
at him as I passed, but paused a hundred feet beyond,
leaned over the broad stone railing, and affected to
study the long vista of Pennsylvania Avenue.

The woman did likewise, at a considerable distance
from me. The tall man excused himself to his companion and went over to her. They talked for several

minutes, but neither of them ever looked in my direction. I could see him gesticulate once or twice, but the dome of the sky has no such acoustic properties as that of Statuary Hall, and I caught none of their words.

Toward the end of their talk he caught her sharply by the arm and leaned over in an attitude that suggested menace. She seemed still and helpless in his hands, looking up into his face as if fascinated. With an abrupt movement he left her and went back to his friend.

I resumed my walk, leading her around the north end of the great building and out across the east plaza, where the curious throngs gather to see men become Presidents. But her talk with the tall man seemed to result in no change of her tactics. She followed, but that was all.

Despite my curiosity, I was getting impatient over the affair. If there was to be a climax, there was no sign of its arrival, or even of its approach. Perhaps I was supposed to go somewhere first. If that was the case, I was perfectly willing to go, for the sake of my own enlightenment; but I had no remote idea what goal I was desired to seek.

I decided to give the golden-domed Congressional Library a chance, and thither I led her at a brisk walk, adopting a change of pace with the idea of letting her know that at last I was set upon a definite mission. She managed to keep up fairly well and was not far behind me when I entered the gorgeously colored lobby of the house of books. But it was all to no purpose; my shadow was merely my shadow.

I resolved to reverse the order of things, and wondered why I had not done it before. She was standing at a window, simulating an interest in the view of the Capitol it afforded, but none the less keeping a close eye on me. It seemed as good an opportunity as any for me to force an acquaintance.

I stepped away suddenly from a study of a wall inscription, and approached the window. She heard me coming, faced me for an instant, and turned away again. I could see her fingers gripping her handbag nervously. There was the same familiar air of uncertainty in her attitude. Strange manners, I thought, for a lady Vidocq! Or was it just another bit of stage business in an incomprehensible play?

"I am looking for some information," I said over her shoulder.

She turned slowly, as if she had expected some speech from me, and regarded me intently with her large brown eyes.

"Information?" she repeated mechanically. Her voice was low-pitched and soft.

"Yes, information," I reëchoed.

She was still holding me in close and grave scrutiny as she said:

"About what?"

"I am trying to learn," I answered, bowing over my

removed hat, "at what date Balboa discovered the Pacific Ocean."

For several seconds she stared at me in amazement. Then I think she must have caught an expression in my eyes, for the gravity in her face vanished, and she burst into a peal of soft, musical laughter.

CHAPTER II

DECIDEDLY charming in moments of mirth, I decided, was this young hunter of men! There was merriment in her eyes as well as laughter upon her lips. She had undergone a sudden transformation as surprising as it was agreeable. It caused me to stare at her in a manner which, under ordinary circumstances, would have passed for rudeness; but I decided I was well entitled to scrutinize, as relentlessly as I pleased, this woman who had some mysterious business with me.

Suddenly she sobered and appeared to consider the point of my inquiry, which had rolled so smoothly from my tongue it astonished me. What put it into my head I have not the least idea, nor had I the faintest desire or need for any information whatever concerning the daring Spaniard who first looked upon the rolling deeps of the mother of all oceans.

"I never was able to pass my history examinations," she answered, with a thoughtful wrinkling of her forehead. "Are you sure it was Balboa?"

"Oh, quite!"

"Somehow, I always get him mixed with De Soto." Her face was grave, but there was a suspicious trembling at the corners of her mouth.

"It was Balboa," I said, with an emphatic nod.

"Vasco Nuñez Balboa—there's the whole name for you."

"Your memory is astonishing," she observed judicially. "Nevertheless, I suspect you are thinking of Vasco da Gama. Didn't he do something?"

"Balboa—for a nickel," I challenged.

"Very well—for a nickel!"

"And it was some time in the sixteenth century."

"The fifteenth," she corrected.

"For another nickel?"

"Done!"

"Now we'll go down to the reading-room and settle it."

As we descended the great marble staircase and made our way to the reference library, I stole two or three glances at her. She went along quite composedly, looking straight ahead; but I suspect she appreciated the complete absurdity of our quest as fully as I.

"This lady," I said to the clerk, "is exceedingly interested in Balboa."

My companion gave me an indignant glance of reproach.

"She would like to know upon what date he discovered the Pacific Ocean," I continued. "Can you tell her?"

"That wasn't fair," she protested, with a slight flush, as the clerk sought a page in a big book. "I haven't the least interest in Balboa."

"But you have money at stake upon it," I reminded her. "Your interest is financial, if not historical."

"September 25, 1513," said the clerk, pushing the big book toward us, with his finger marking a line.

"The sixteenth century," I commented gravely.

"Certainly," replied the clerk.

As we walked away from the desk, she opened her envelope-shaped bag and found a dime among the coins in its central compartment. I noted her femininity as she took a cursory glance at her face in the mirror inside the bag's flap, and pursed her lips as she made a dab or two at the waves of hair beneath her cloche before she snapped the bag to. She handed me the dime.

"Thank you," I said, as I dropped it into my pocket. "That was cheap for such an important piece of knowledge."

"Important!" she echoed, as we strolled toward the entrance. "Do you mean to tell me you consider it important?"

"To be frank, I have forgotten the date already," I answered promptly.

She stole a swift glance at me, and burst into laughter.

"A very foolish and futile quest!" she declared when her mirth slackened.

"By no means," I assured her. "In some histories, you know, it is recorded that Balboa, immediately following his discovery, sat down and ate lunch."

"Nonsense!"

"But let's assume that he did. It won't damage history. He must have been furiously hungry after climbing all those mountains. Now, why not emulate Balboa?"

She gave me a sidelong glance of inquiry, with a slight lifting of her eyebrows.

"And eat lunch," I added.

"But we haven't discovered anything!"

"Yet we may. It can't be possible that all has been discovered. We can at least discover the lunch."

She drew her lips together doubtfully and appeared to consider.

"And I'm hungry," I added. "I haven't climbed any mountains, but I've walked much."

She looked at me sharply, colored faintly, and quickly withdrew her glance.

"Have you a choice of restaurants?" I asked as we descended the library steps.

"Not when I'm as hungry as a bear," she confessed.

Well, I was giving her the opportunity she sought. If she had played me adroitly, so as to reverse the positions of pursuer and pursued, I did not care particularly. What I could not fathom was her reluctance and hesitation, which only vanished during her moments of amusement. Unless it was a studied part of the play, I could see no reason for her manner.

I had most obligingly assisted her in performing the first part of her errand—a task which seemed to be giving her much perplexity. She knew, of course, that I had been aware of her pursuit, but she could scarcely suspect I had overheard the instructions upon which she was acting.

While we were waiting for a taxi, I began to form a new opinion of women detectives. Here was a woman of evident breeding engaged in a business of which my notion had never been exalted. This, perhaps, argued that the mission on which she was engaged was a matter of high importance—which puzzled me greatly. How was I concerned in it? What did I know that the tall man wanted to know?

I was curious to see how this agent of his would go about the remainder of her quest. She seemed to be in no hurry. At first I had set her down as no more than an amateur in the business; now I began to conclude that, even if an amateur, she was decidedly clever —a mistress of dissimulation.

Only once on the way downtown did she make reference to our prolonged exploration of the Capitol.

"You saw me at the Capitol?" she ventured.

I concluded she was anxious to learn just how much I knew concerning her errand.

"Come to think of it, I believe I passed you twice," I answered in a tone of assumed carelessness.

She must have known I was telling much less than the whole truth; but I think my reply relieved her a bit, as indicating I intended to make no reference to past events. She did not speak of the matter again, nor did I urge it, quite willing to let her follow her own method.

If she had a method, it was beautifully indirect. We talked about everything save that which overwhelmingly concerned us both. She was bright and whimsical, with a quick sense of humor, particularly a sense of the absurd; yet there was nothing shallow or superficial about her mind.

I found her more interesting in serious moments than in her occasional bursts of gayety. I would catch a grave, thoughtful expression in her face, her great brown eyes gazing in a detached way at something they did not appear to see. She would rouse herself from these periods of preoccupation with a little shrug when she found me studying her, usually supplementing it with some casual question concerning the nearest object of interest that presented itself.

Once she asked me if I was a lawyer. When I replied in the negative, she relapsed into another spell of silence. The tall man, who evidently knew who I was, must have been aware of the fact that I was not of the legal profession, but had not supplied her with the information.

"I can only offer you the advice of a layman," I said.

"Do you know anything about wills?" she asked abruptly.

"Not the least thing. I never made one, and I never got anything out of one. Why? Are you making your will?"

This struck her as amusing, for she laughed, but did not explain. Her laugh pleased me. It was low and melodious, like a soothing chord of music; just the sort of laugh that harmonized with her voice. A strident laugh in a woman annoys me. Hers was mellow, soft and smooth.

Though I knew she was playing a part, there was one quality about her which unobtrusively impressed itself upon me as genuine. She had the birth and breeding of a gentlewoman. What I could not reconcile with this was the fact that she was engaged in an adventure, if it might be so called, upon which no gentlewoman, under circumstances easily conceivable, would embark.

And the tall man! He seemed utterly incongruous when I studied this slender, charming, aristocratic young woman at my side.

I decided to let the situation work itself out in its own way, having already taken all the initiative I proposed to assume.

The restaurant we entered was one of the popular lunch resorts of the Washington hotel district, but the usual midday rush was over, and we had no difficulty in obtaining a table in a quiet corner of the room. There she pleased me again, for she ordered what she wanted promptly and without hesitation. I am not clever at ordering luncheons for women; it bothers me when they pore over the menu card as if they were considering the problem from the financial aspect, and then appeal to my own unimaginative mind for suggestions. This woman knew what she wanted, and she asked for it without making a preliminary study of prices.

One of the many vagaries of male vanity, as I have studied it, is pleasure at being discovered in some public place with a pretty woman. Perhaps it is a trait inherited from our aboriginal ancestors, modified by time and convention, yet still expressing in a feeble way man's exultation over capture and possession. I was flattering myself with this sentiment when I chanced to glance about the room and my eye fell upon a party of three women seated at a table not far distant.

I blushed hotly, like a schoolboy trapped deep in guilt by his teacher. It must have been a peculiarly obvious blush, for my companion noted it with an appraising glance, and asked:

"Is anything the matter?"

"Not at all," I answered quickly. "It just seems a little warm in here."

But there was something the matter—very much the matter. One of the three women who were just finishing their lunches was Miss Fenwick; and Jeanette Fenwick and I were engaged to be married.

Here was an encounter upon which I had not calculated. That Jeanette had seen me was beyond doubt. That she knew no more of the identity of my companion than I did myself was also probably true. That she must have recognized in her, however, an exceedingly attractive young woman was above dispute.

Of course, there was absolutely nothing wrong in the situation. It was no grave offense, I take it, for a man to take a woman to lunch, particularly when he makes not the least attempt to conceal the fact. And when Jeanette Fenwick knew the reason in this particular instance, there could be no misunderstanding.

Yet I did not like the expression on Jeanette's face.

She did not meet my eyes at all, and I confess I made no effort to intercept a glance from her. One of the women with her was her mother; the other I did not know. Mrs. Fenwick was of some social importance, and with it she had a certain severity of manner and a rather restricted viewpoint. If there was to be any deliberate misunderstanding of my attitude toward the young woman in brown, I knew it would take deep and firm root in the mind of Mrs. Fenwick.

It would be easier to explain things to Jeanette than to her mother. But even Jeanette, in the swift glance I gave her, did not seem to be in a mood receptive to explanations.

Once or twice again I looked toward the other table, so that I might not subsequently be accused of trying to avoid a recognition; but Jeanette was engaged in animated conversation with her mother. Her failure to see me was too obvious, I thought; it made me vaguely uncomfortable.

The only person whose eye I caught was the woman who was a stranger to me, and she gave me a frank, expressionless stare, finally turning her eyes upon my companion and favoring her with a long, comprehensive study. I was convinced then I was a subject for conversation at the other table. Fortunately, I thought, the girl in brown was seated with her back toward Mrs. Fenwick and her party, and would be spared the embarrassment of scrutiny.

If Jeanette had looked at me as they left their table, I would have welcomed the opportunity to speak to her; but the trio swept from the restaurant without even turning their heads in our direction. It was easy enough to read a meaning into their manner.

I flushed, and the girl with me saw it. She turned in her chair to learn the cause. Her eyes dwelt for a moment upon the three retreating figures. When she looked back at me, I was quite certain she had sensed something of the situation.

"Friends?" she remarked.

"Oh, yes—friends," I replied carelessly.

"You did not bow to them," she suggested, after a pause.

"Why—er—no, I didn't. The fact is, they didn't bow to me."

"Oh!"

I thought there was the flicker of a smile on her lips. Certainly there was a glint of amusement in her eyes. But she did not further allude to the matter.

I was moody and irritated over the incident for some time. The mere conduct of Jeanette and her mother, the marked way in which they ignored my presence, conveyed an accusation I thought, and knew, was unjust. It was not until my companion began to chatter of a recent experience in a balky automobile that I roused myself from unpleasant preoccupation and gave my mind to the problem in hand.

Luncheon had brought us no nearer to the object of her errand, so far as I could see, and I was becoming impatient. She never came to the point at all; nor did she, so far as I could interrupt her conversation, even hint at it. She asked no questions concerning myself or my business, and volunteered no information about herself.

She never spoke of the tall man, and in such persons as she did mention, I could recognize none who seemed to fit his description. From time to time I kept a lookout for him, to see if he, in turn, followed us; but he had evidently left the matter entirely to her after his final instructions on the west front of the Capitol.

As the afternoon grew late, the nervousness of manner I had observed in her earlier in the day returned. I imagined she was becoming perplexed and annoyed at her failure to make any headway. At least, that was the only way I could interpret her conduct.

She seemed to be in an entirely passive mood, assenting readily to any suggestions I made, and venturing none of her own. We strolled through the Mall, went into the National Museum for a while, talking about matters that were not uppermost in the minds of either of us, each furtively watching the other for a sign, a gesture, a word, that might lead toward some sort of a climax.

I did not make the slightest effort to help her out of her difficulties. I was as much consumed by curiosity as ever, yet was resolved that the next move in this apparently purposeless puzzle should be hers.

Finally it came. We were on the avenue, walking slowly back toward the Capitol, and there had been a considerable period of silence on both sides, accompanied by visibly growing agitation in her manner.

She seemed as if she were continually on the point of bursting out with some exclamation, yet always checking it on her lips.

"Will you do me a favor?" she asked suddenly.

"Of course," I replied.

There was excitement in her eyes, a faint quaver in her voice. I wondered if this was more acting.

"You will think it a very extraordinary request," she went on.

Would I? I was not so sure about that. The whole affair had been extraordinary to me.

"Please make it," I said.

"It will take your whole evening," she pursued. Still the same queer reluctance to get down to facts.

"I have no engagements. My evening is at your disposal."

Why shouldn't it be? I still had as much to learn as she; in truth, more. For she knew who I was, and I had not the least notion who she was.

"I want you to act as my escort."

"I shall be honored," I said, bowing.

She paused again until we had covered another half block.

"Do you mind wearing full dress?" was her next question.

"Not at all," I said, laughing a little.

"Can you be ready at about nine o'clock?"

I nodded.

"Make it nine-thirty," she amended, after a moment's thought.

"Certainly. Where shall I call for you?"

This at first seemed to be a problem for her, but at last she replied:

"You cannot call for me. Oh, I know it sounds quite irregular; but please don't ask me why! You will have to meet me."

"All right; I'll meet you. Where?"

"Anywhere will do."

"How about here, then?" I suggested.

We were at Twelfth and the avenue.

"Yes," she assented, with a nod. "Here, at nine-thirty."

It flashed through my mind that this might be the termination of the whole incident; yet I could not conceive her having made such an unusual request if she was not sincere. She evidently divined my thought, for she asked quickly:

"Are you afraid I may not keep the appointment?"

"I was considering that possibility," I confessed.

"But I will keep it," she went on hurriedly. "I shall be here at nine-thirty. You may be absolutely sure of that."

"I no longer have any doubts," I said gravely. "Shall we need a car?"

"I will have one," she answered. "And now, good afternoon—and thank you!"

She gave me her hand for an instant, and then stepped toward the curb to hail a passing taxi. It was clear I was not to follow her further, although she did not in so many words ask me to leave her.

As the taxi drew up, and I prepared to assist her into it, I said suddenly:

"May I ask where we are going?"

She hesitated, then leaned toward me from inside the taxi and said, in a low tone:

"To the White House!"

The door swung shut, and the car moved off down the avenue. I stood staring after it for a full minute, a vision in my mind of a slender, brown-clad figure, leaning forward and almost whispering a sentence that astonished me as much as any event of the past several hours.

To the White House!

What business had I at the White House—or she?

I had an almost overpowering impulse to pursue the disappearing car and compel the woman of mystery to tell me more. Yet I knew, too, down in my heart, that she would not fail me. And I felt, as strongly as I could feel anything, that here was an adventure that was just upon the threshold.

"To the White House for you, Dan Mansfield," I said, half aloud, as I swung about and started off at a brisk walk. "With a pretty girl! And you don't even know her name. Careful, my boy, careful!"

CHAPTER III

A FULL quarter of an hour before the time fixed by the girl in brown found me pacing slowly back and forth at the place we had designated. My thoughts were in a chaotic state, yet I was calm enough; for although I could not obtain a glimmer, as yet, of what it was all about, I was prepared to accept any kind of development with equanimity—or, at any rate, I believed I was.

It had not been difficult to learn that at the White House that evening there was an official reception in honor of a visiting Swedish prince, and that, if the evening was fair, the grounds as well as the dignified old mansion itself would be open for the entertainment of guests. Evidently my companion of the afternoon was supplied with invitations, for I had none. Why she was so anxious to go to the White House, if her business concerned me, was beyond my ability even to guess. Perhaps I was to be displayed for the benefit of some person also in the employment and confidence of the tall man; perhaps the tall man himself would be there.

I shrugged my shoulders in an attempt to affect indifference, but did not greatly deceive myself. I was not indifferent; I was eaten with curiosity and bewilderment.

As I swung about at one end of my self-appointed post of sentry duty, a taxi rolled smoothly up to the curb at my side and came to a halt. I saw a white hand rest for an instant on the ledge of the opened window and make a single gesture. The girl in brown was punctual to the minute.

But she was no longer the girl in brown. The taxi was of that type fitted with a lighting appliance which lights the interior of the car when the door is open and is automatically switched off on its closing. Stepping in, I delayed the closing of the door long enough to obtain a look at my companion.

An evening wrap of gorgeous silver brocade with a huge collar of white fox fur was thrown about her shoulders, yet remained unfastened at the throat, so that I could see beneath it a softly clinging gown of white georgette, as I believe they call it. There was a delicate platinum chain about her throat, with a pendant pearl that glowed softly in the light. Just what it was she wore over her hair I am unable to say; it was some sort of a feminine ornament like a silver fillet bound about the undulating smoothness of her permanently waved bob which I had guessed, from the glimpse I had had of it from beneath her tight-fitting cloche hat of the afternoon, would be as it was. The silver thing about her hair lent an almost coquettish appearance to her small head. Of one thing I was sure—she was amazingly attractive.

She replied to my scrutiny with a smile; then I closed the door and we were in comparative darkness.

The taxi moved up the avenue in the direction of the White House.

For a moment neither of us spoke. The richness of her attire had surprised me; yet I scarcely knew why, for that afternoon, in her brown and tans and mink coat, I had recognized her as a handsomely gowned woman. Perhaps it was the incongruity of her business that gave rise to my momentary astonishment.

"You are prompt," I said at length, for want of a better remark.

"That is praise," she answered, with a soft laugh.

We were rounding the corner of the Treasury building before I could think of anything else to say. Then I asked:

"Have you cards?"

"Of course. I'm not quite a burglar, you know."

I felt that she was smiling at me.

"Shall I take them?"

Her response was hurried.

"No; it isn't necessary—if you don't mind."

She did not want me to see the cards. Evidently I was not to get her name in that fashion.

"I don't mind at all," I answered, although I knew it was rather unusual for a woman guest to present cards at the door, rather than her escort.

We turned from Executive Avenue into the carriage gate that leads to the east portico, and a White House footman opened the door. She had handed her cards of invitation to an attendant, so that I caught not a glimpse of them, and then I was removing her wrap to hand it to one of the checkers.

As I saw her, standing straight and slender in her white gown, I could hardly repress an exclamation of admiration. Who she was I knew not, and at that moment I did not care. All I knew was that my companion was one of the fairest and most alluring figures I had ever seen at a White House function. I was proud of her. I think she caught the meaning of the glance I gave her, for she flushed faintly and seemed by no means displeased.

"We are early guests," I said, as we ascended the staircase to the main floor.

She responded only with a nod and we went into the East Room. Here the comparatively small crowd bore witness to the truth of my observation; the company was just beginning to arrive. I saw her glancing about the room expectantly, in fact, almost fearfully, and wondered if she were looking for the tall man.

It was quite obvious my companion was attracting attention. Women engaged in conversation with their escorts would stop abruptly as we passed, turn, and look after her. Men paid her the tribute of frankly approving eyes. She did not appear to be conscious of this, but I never lost an incident of it. It flattered me. Yet I could not put from my mind a sense of embarrassment. I knew many people in Washington; it was more than likely I should meet some of them here. If it came to a matter of introductions, what was I to do? She was a complete stranger.

"As it is so early," I suggested, "why not try the lawns for a while? It is quite pleasant."

"Certainly," she assented.

We made our way through the Blue Room and reached the porch. The newly-leaved trees scattered about the wide stretch of greensward within the grounds were glowing with colored lights, and a white beam from a powerful searchlight was focused on the fountain so that the jets of water glistened like a shower of diamonds. Out into this park of beauty we went, her hand resting lightly on my arm.

"Will you please tell me what I am to do?" I asked suddenly.

"Do?"

"Yes. It is somewhat confusing, you know. Who am I supposed to be?"

"Why, you are my escort," she said lightly, glancing at me with a smile. "Isn't that sufficient?"

"Not only sufficient, but a distinct compliment," I answered. "And yet—"

"What does an escort usually do?" she broke in, laughing. "Must I instruct you?"

"In this case, I'm afraid you must, Miss—"

It was the first suggestion I had made of a desire to learn her identity, but she swept it aside as if she had not noticed it.

"You are a little barbaric, I fear," she declared as we went down the long stretch of lawn toward the fountain. "If you really must be told, why—my escort is supposed to talk to me, to keep me amused, to bring me some refreshment, if I want it; to dance with me occasionally, to see that I am not a wallflower, to make himself agreeable, to run errands—"

"You will never be a wallflower," I interrupted; "not if I stood you against the wall and left you there."

"Many thanks—many!" she exclaimed, with a sweeping curtsey. "That was excellent; you are not a barbarian, after all. I think you need no further instruction in your duties."

I think I have remarked that she had a keen sense of the absurd. I heard her laughing softly and, turning, saw her watching a tiny, strutting, dark-visaged foreign attaché, enveloped in a resplendent gold-laced uniform, a sword dangling at his heels, with an exceedingly large woman leaning upon his arm and looking foolishly proud in her possession. I could not restrain a smile myself. The little man had a quick ear, for he caught the low laughter, turned his head quickly, and frowned heavily.

"You'll bring about international complications if you're not careful," I warned.

"Let's fly!" she whispered, and, catching about her the flimsy scarf she had about her shoulders, she raced down the lawn.

Perforce, I followed, but was obliged to pause in my pursuit to dig up her big fan of feathers, which she dropped in her mad flight. Twenty yards beyond me she stopped and turned to see what delayed me. A rose-colored beam from the searchlight began to roam the grounds, uncertainly, hesitatingly, until it fell upon her and became fixed. She was standing quite alone against a dark background of trees, and in the rosy light she looked like some beautiful, flaming lily.

For several seconds I think she was unconscious of the almost startling picture she made; then I heard a murmur of low comment from persons near me, which presently reached her. With a little cry of dismay she turned and started to flee.

I caught her, brought her down to a walk, and we sought a refuge of comparative seclusion, the searchlight with the rose-red beam following us until a friendly evergreen intervened.

"Oh!" she exclaimed, "I could murder that man with the light!"

"And the President's guests could bless him," I added.

But not again could I lure her out upon the lawn where the searchlight played. Slowly and circuitously we wandered back to the White House, where the crowd was becoming dense. The receiving party was on the south porch, and a line of several hundred persons had formed to perform the perfunctory and wearisome duty of meeting the guest of honor.

"Shall we get into the line?" I asked.

"It's tiresome, I think," she answered.

The Swedish prince had not the slightest attraction for me, and we strolled around to the north front of the house. There was a crowd inside as we entered, and we paused under the shelter of a palm grove in the great hall, listening to an orchestra that had begun to play for the dancers.

I heard an exclamation from two women who came out from the East Room, and saw them run toward us.

"Mary! You little fraud!"

It was the elder of the pair who cried out joyously, and she clasped my companion in a warm embrace. The younger woman awaited her turn impatiently, and promptly duplicated the greeting when an opportunity offered.

Neither of the newcomers had at first looked at me, but with one accord they turned and smiled frankly at me. I caught my companion's eye for a fleeting instant, and saw in it an expression of fright and dismay. Her lips were compressed tightly, and she had raised one hand to her breast as if to ward off a blow. She shook her head as if tossing off some incubus, and smiled.

"And this, of course, is Mr. Vinton," said the elder of the strangers, stepping forward and reaching out her hand with cordial energy.

Rather mechanically I took it and bowed. She pumped at my arm vigorously.

"You're not in the least as I pictured you," she exclaimed, studying my face with a curiosity which was not meant, of course, to be offensive, but which was exceedingly embarrassing to me, nevertheless.

I bowed again, and forced a smile.

"And I congratulate you most sincerely."

"Why, thank you," I answered.

I could think of nothing else to say; I was fast becoming dazed.

"You have a charming and beautiful wife, Mr. Vinton."

It was like some fantastic dream. The words seemed to be coming from a long distance, yet they were clear and distinct—and overwhelming!

A wife! *I* had a wife! And my name was Vinton!

I stared at the woman blankly, and she laughed merrily in my face, mistaking my expression, I imagine, for clumsy shyness. Consternation was the only emotion I experienced; then I felt resentment and anger slowly succeeding. What sort of a trick was this that was being played upon me?

I looked beyond the woman who was holding my hand into the eyes of the girl who had led me into the trap. Never had I seen such an expression of pitiful appeal in human eyes. Her lips were quivering. She was leaning slightly toward me, her body rigid as a statue, her hands clenched together, her cheeks, beneath their slight touch of rouge, pale as her white gown. She was pleading silently; I verily believe she was praying.

My rising anger vanished in bewilderment. I began to wonder if I was really sane; it was all like a grotesque delusion. I pulled myself together in some fashion. At least, I would not appear ridiculous; I would wait until the reckoning.

I tried to assume an air of ease, although I could

feel the blood racing hotly in my temples, and knew
my face was flushed a deep red.

"She is all you say—and more," I stammered.

Mary—they had called her Mary—stepped forward
like a woman suddenly awakened from a trance.

"This is Mrs. McCutcheon, Robert," she said, laying her hand with an air of gentle ownership upon my
arm.

So I was Robert Vinton! Well, at least it was a
comfort to know my full name.

"I am charmed to know you, Mrs. McCutcheon," I
said, in a steadier voice. "Mary has spoken of you
often."

I felt a soft pressure of the girl's fingers on my
arm as she reached out her free hand and drew the
younger woman toward me.

"And this, Robert, is her daughter, Mrs. Pratt."

Once more I went through the experience of being
felicitated upon the possession of a lovely wife.

"Mother and I have been so anxious to see you!"
exclaimed the woman called Mrs. Pratt. "We didn't
even know you were really engaged, so you can imagine
how surprised we were when we received announcement cards!"

"Yes?" I said, smiling.

"Yes, indeed! I never believed Mary could be so
sly and mysterious."

I did. I knew it; but I did not say so to Mrs.
Pratt.

"We knew that Mary was in the West, and that you

were also there," she rattled on; "but we hadn't the least idea it would be so soon. Why, it seems almost like an elopement!"

"We hadn't thought of it that way," I laughed. "Had we, dear?"

I deliberately turned to Mary as I said "dear," and looked at her challengingly. Her cheeks colored quickly, and I could feel her hand trembling. She slipped her arm within mine, smiled sweetly at me, and met my challenge with one of her own.

"It wasn't an elopement, of course," she said to Mrs. McCutcheon. "But Robert is just a large, foolish boy, with a streak of romance and a horror of formalities. So I humored him."

She threw her head to one side with a pretty gesture as she said this and looked up at me—the little fiend! Her eyes were shining with mischief. Two minutes before she had been a picture of mental anguish and terror. Never had I seen such a transformation.

"So you are enjoying it, my lady," I thought. "Perhaps two can play at it!"

"But *please* tell us all about it!" cried Mrs. Pratt, impatiently. "What sort of a wedding was it?"

"You'll laugh when you hear," I said.

I felt Mary clutching at my sleeve, but refused to look at her.

"Now, Robert, please—"

I interrupted her remorselessly.

"We were married in the pilot house of an old-fashioned steamboat," I said, with a cheerful grin at Mrs. McCutcheon.

"Oh!"

The exclamation was from Mary. She forgot to say "Robert." I looked at her triumphantly. The two women stared at me incredulously, then at Mary.

"Really?" cried Mrs. Pratt, when she had recovered speech.

I nodded and laughed.

"Mary, dear, you may as well tell them," I added.

I was gloating; I would teach this Mary to play a joke. But she recovered herself amazingly, and fairly put me to shame with what followed. With blushing reluctance, laughter, and a wealth of nimble invention, she told the prettiest and most entertaining story imaginable, concerning a runaway couple seeking to escape the tortures of a church wedding, fleeing aboard a Western river-steamer, being pursued by a party of merry conspirators and a minister, and cornered willy-nilly in the pilot-house and married out of hand, before they had a chance to protest.

I marveled at the tale. In fact, so glib was it, so replete with details—yes, even with names—that I began to wonder if Mary really had been married to somebody under such extraordinary circumstances.

When she had concluded it she shot a glance of victory and warning at me that went home.

"Every word of it is true," I assented, with a solemn nod.

"How perfectly wonderful!" This was from the daughter.

"Mary!" A single word was all that Mrs. Mc-Cutcheon could say.

And I heard a gentle whisper, close to my ear:

"That's for Balboa!"

I understood. The affair of the library was avenged. I began to think my lady's wit was dangerous to tempt.

We talked with her friends for a while, promising to call and meet some other members of the family, until Mary began to drag me firmly away.

"I suppose you'll be taking her back to England very soon," said the elder woman ruefully, as she shook hands again.

It appeared that I was from England, too.

"Quite soon, I'm afraid," I answered.

When they had disappeared in the direction of the Blue Room I turned and looked at Mary. She met my look timidly, nervously playing with her fan. I noticed it was broken. All the ease and animation had suddenly gone from her. She was pale; her eyes were serious and troubled.

"I think we'll go inside and have a talk," I said, taking her by the arm.

She shrank back from me as if I were going to strike her.

"No! No!" she pleaded.

I could feel her trembling in my grasp.

"But, my dear girl," I said, "this matter—"

"Not now! Wait! Oh, please wait!"

"You'll admit I'm entitled to an explanation, won't you?"

She bit her lip and seemed to be on the brink of tears.

"Yes—but wait. I—I can't explain now. Won't you be merciful—for a little while?"

Her big dark eyes were piteous as she raised them to mine. I was weak, and I relented.

"Let's get a glass of punch," I said.

Amid the chattering, laughing, pushing crowd that surged about the refreshment-tables as if they were so many bargain counters, she had, to all outward appearance, completely recovered her spirits, and was as gay and unconcerned as any of the company. She gave me no time for reflection, scarcely any for words; she was as voluble as a magpie, hurrying from one topic to another bewilderingly, coining little verbal caricatures of persons she saw, and discussing inconsequential things with as much earnestness and animation as if they were matters of grave moment. Yet underneath it all I could detect a high nervous tension, an overwhelming desire to divert her own mind, as well as mine. She was making a desperate effort to forget and to make me forget.

Not for one moment would she permit me to take her out of the throng. I suggested another stroll on the lawn, where the Marine Band was playing, but she found some excuse. She suspected, I think, that I intended to question her, and she proposed to give me no opportunity.

It was while making our way slowly through the main hall toward the Blue Room that I received another shock.

A young lieutenant of the army, in full-dress uniform, stepped in front of her, halted, and bowed smilingly.

She looked at him with swift recognition, uttered an exclamation of pleasure, and extended her hand cordially.

"Lieutenant Ferris!" she cried. "It's fine to see you. I thought you were still in the Philippines."

"Oh, they don't sentence us for life," he said, with a laugh. "I've been back since January."

"And Captain Holbrook?"

"Still mingling with the Moros, poor fellow," he answered. "But his relief will come soon. How is your sister Fay?"

"Never better. She mentions you sometimes when she writes."

"Abroad, then, I take it."

"Oh, yes. She's a natural-born foreigner, if you can say that of an American."

He was trying to catch a glimpse of her left hand which was covered by her fan as he remarked:

"When I said 'Miss Donaldson' I did not know whether it was still correct or not."

"Yes, indeed," she answered, laughing. Then, with

a sudden apology, she turned to me. "This is Mr. Larned, Lieutenant Ferris," she said.

"Glad to know you, sir," he responded heartily, grasping my hand.

I mumbled something intended as a greeting, and dumbly awaited the next shock.

Miss Donaldson! Mr. Larned! Two brand new sets of names within a quarter of an hour! Was it a burlesque, a nightmare, or what? Was she crazy, or I?

She seemed to have no fear I would not play the part, as she had had on our encounter with Mrs. McCutcheon and her daughter, for she did not glance at me after the introduction, but entered into a lively conversation with the young officer that consisted mostly of reminiscences.

"A resident of Washington, Mr. Larned?" he asked me, as he prepared to take his departure.

"Occasionally," I replied, as we shook hands again.

"A sort of an American nomad," the girl supplemented; I know not why, unless it was for the sake of making conversation. "Well, good-by, Lieutenant Ferris. I congratulate you on your release from bondage."

I halted her rather forcibly when we had moved a few paces from him, and whispered angrily:

"For Heaven's sake, what is the meaning of all this?"

"Not now!" she answered, trying to urge me forward.

"But I will know—Mrs. Vinton, Miss Donaldson—whoever you are. It must end right here!"

"No, no, no!" Again she was quivering with apprehension.

"But listen! I—"

"I beg you!"

There was something in the girl's eyes that made an easy victim of me. I made a gesture of despair as she took my arm and led me into the Blue Room.

"I'd like to dance," she said. "Will you please ask me?"

"Why, certainly," I said, with a short laugh. "May I have this dance—Mary?"

For answer, she gave me an amused nod, and I made a passage for her through the cordon of onlookers that stood three and four deep about the dancers. The orchestra had refrained from jazz, for a wonder, and was playing a waltz.

I am not fond of dancing, as a rule, and care little or nothing for most of the modern dances, but I can waltz, and my partner was a revelation. She was exquisitely graceful. So lightly and surely did she move I could scarcely feel that my arm circled her waist. It was like dancing with a beautiful phantom. That she was attracting an unwonted amount of attention I could see with half a glance. The old feeling of self-flattery mounted within me.

As I led her from the floor we came face to face, on the threshold of the Blue Room, with Jeanette Fenwick! Her hand was resting on the arm of the young officer to whom I had been introduced but a few minutes before.

The color mounted to my face as our glances met, and involuntarily I opened my lips to speak. The words died on them when I saw not the slightest sign of recognition in her glance. She bestowed a swift look at my companion; then she stepped aside to make room for us to pass.

"We meet again, Mr. Larned," said the lieutenant, with a genial nod as we went by them.

And Jeanette heard—I knew it, although she did not for an instant betray a sign of emotion or surprise.

Mary glanced inquiringly at me, and asked, after a moment's pause:

"Isn't she one of those three women we saw in the restaurant this afternoon?"

"She is," I said stonily.

"I thought you said you knew her?"

"I do."

"But she saw you. She looked directly at you."

"Yes."

"Then why—has anything happened? Who is she?"

"She is a Miss Fenwick," and added, rather brutally, "that is her real name, too!"

"If I have done anything—"

"Nothing," I broke in. I was too angry for much speech.

"Yet it seemed as if she deliberately ignored you," she went on persistently.

Would she never stop? Was this part of the errand upon which the tall man had despatched her? Well, I would satisfy her, then!

"If it will explain matters at all," I said sharply, "Miss Fenwick and I are engaged to be married—and you have led me into a fine mess."

I heard her catch her breath, but for a full minute she did not speak. Then it was in a subdued and frightened voice:

"I am sorry—so sorry! Please take me away, now."

We went downstairs to the cloak-room, neither of us speaking. As I placed her luxurious wrap about her shoulders I could feel her trembling. She steadily avoided meeting my glance, and seemed anxious to escape from the place which had been the scene of three bewildering meetings.

For my own part, I was more than glad to go. I wanted no more chance encounters; but I did want an opportunity to demand an explanation that would cover everything from the moment of the overheard whisper.

I heard her murmuring to herself as we went to the carriage entrance, and, inclining my head slightly, heard the words:

"I cannot do it! I cannot!"

I gave the attendant the number of our car, and after a short wait, the taxi drew up under the porte-cochère. As the door was opened, the girl stepped forward and said something in a low tone to the chauffeur, who nodded and touched his cap. I handed her in, but, as I was about to place my foot on the running board, she reached out her hand and swiftly drew shut the door.

"Good-by—and forgive me!" she said in a tense voice, leaning forward so that I could see her pallor.

The taxi swung down the driveway, leaving me standing on the White House steps.

CHAPTER IV

I WAS so dismayed and chagrined as to become stupefied. I stood staring after the vanishing car as if beholding such a vehicle for the first time in my life. Not until it had reached the end of the curving driveway and turned south into Executive Avenue did I stir from my place on the steps.

Then, with an involuntary cry, I leaped forward in pursuit. I did not turn my head to see what the White House footman thought of the matter, and cared not for the little crowd of guests who were waiting for cars. I sprinted wildly down the short stretch of macadam and along the sidewalk in the direction of Pennsylvania Avenue.

A long row of waiting taxis, drawn up along the curb, obstructed my view of the disappearing quarry, and I dashed through an opening between two of them and took to the middle of the street. I could see the tail-light of the girl's taxi ahead of me, and I had not gone a quarter of a block before I realized it was rapidly distancing me.

Yet I ran on, hopelessly, spurred forward by the mad desire to overtake, just as a man will set out in futile pursuit of a train he knows he cannot reach.

The taxi crossed the avenue and rolled smoothly northward. As I reached the corner I slackened my

57

pace and looked about me for some more effective means of pursuit. I was conscious of several persons staring at me, but I cared nothing for that. My whole mind was concentrated on one object.

On across the avenue I ran, eluding a passing trolley by inches, only to find myself directly in front of a motorcycle. The rider of it jammed his brakes with a cry, brought it to a stop, and dropped one foot to the pavement to steady himself. He wore the uniform of a messenger-boy.

"Here!" I cried, seizing him by the shoulder and giving him a push that forced him to dismount.

He gasped at me—a breathless gentleman in evening dress. I thrust a hand into one of my pockets and drew forth some bills.

"Take this!" I exclaimed.

It was a twenty I handed him. Mechanically he took the money from my hand and stood staring dumbly.

"I'll notify your office where the machine is," I gasped.

Wresting the handle-bars from his grasp, I gave the machine a push forward and threw myself into the saddle. He had not stopped the engine when he halted to avoid a collision with me, and all I had to do was to throw in the clutch. I had had some experience with motorcycles, and, while I was not familiar with this particular make, I found it responded quickly to my touch.

Heading up Madison street, which skirts Lafayette Park on the east side, I turned on full speed and blazed a reckless path through a number of machines waiting for theater patrons. I never cast a glance behind me, but heard the owner of the motorcycle shouting until his voice was lost in the distance.

I slowed down as I approached the H street crossing. The broad sweep of Vermont Avenue that stretched ahead of me was empty of vehicles. As I cast a swift look up H street I saw the tail-light of a car swing around the corner of Sixteenth street and disappear. I headed after it. Turning into Sixteenth I saw the car a short block ahead of me. I drew up on it until half that distance separated us, and slowed down to an equal pace.

In every outward aspect it was the same taxi which had conveyed the girl and myself to the White House; yet I could not be absolutely sure, for all the cars belonging to that company were painted alike, and I had taken no notice of the license number. To add to my uncertainty, I had for several seconds lost sight of the object of my pursuit while commandeering the machine I bestrode. Yet no other taxi was in sight, and I followed hopefully.

I felt grim and angry, and I was much excited. The girl had played me the shabbiest kind of a trick—luring me on a thoroughly purposeless errand and exhibiting me to official society in the guise of a fool. I knew no more of her than I did the first moment I set eyes on her, while she, for some reason utterly beyond my guess, had suddenly interrupted or abandoned the business which had set her on my trail.

Sixteenth street was nearly empty as taxi and pursuer rolled quietly uptown into the smart residence section of the Northwest. The taxi skirted the circle at Massachusetts Avenue and kept onward. I followed as closely as I thought advisable, for I did not wish to warn the driver or the occupant of the car that chase had been given.

For the better part of a mile our course was a straight one. Then I was suddenly aware I was rapidly closing in on the taxi, which was drawing in toward the curb on the west side of the street. I shut off power and brought the motorcycle to an abrupt standstill. Dismounting, I leaned it against a tree, and stepped behind the same shelter.

The taxi stopped. Breathless, I stood in the dark shadows and waited.

The door of the taxi opened and the girl in the shimmery silver brocade coat stepped out. I heaved a deep sigh of satisfaction; she had not succeeded in evading me. She stood motionless under the glare of a nearby street lamp, looking up at a tall, dark dwelling, in front of which the taxi had halted. She turned and crossed the sidewalk briskly, pushed open an iron gate, crossed the courtyard, and ran up the stone steps.

At the top of them she stopped, and I judged she was ringing the bell, for now and then she stepped back and looked upward at the windows. I could see no light there.

Presently she glanced up and down the street as if

expectant. She rang the bell again, but it brought no response. I saw her head bent close over something; she stooped in front of the door and seemed to be thrusting that something under it. Rising quickly, she made a final survey of the lonely street in both directions, ran swiftly down the steps, clanged the courtyard gate behind her, spoke to the taxi driver, and disappeared within the shelter of the cab.

It started off in a long curve, so as to head downtown. As it passed the spot where I was standing I edged slowly around the tree to avoid any possible chance of being observed. I hesitated between pursuit and a consuming desire to know whether she had left a message on the doorstep. I decided to attempt both.

The darkened house was not more than thirty or forty yards from me, and I sprinted for it. Leaping up the steps three at a time, I dropped to my knees and brought my eyes close to the threshold of the carved outer doors. A tiny triangle of white projected less than a quarter of an inch. I clutched at it with a thumb and forefinger, but only succeeded in pushing it further in. With an exclamation of annoyance, I turned and glanced down the street while I felt in my pocket for a pen-knife. The tail-light of the taxi was visible nearly two blocks away; there was desperate need of haste.

Opening a blade of my knife I struck a match and bent to my task again. The corner of a white card was just visible. Carefully, and as steadily as I could,

I slipped the knife blade beneath the door and impaled the card on its sharp point; but my hand was shaking as I attempted to draw it forth, and the card was released.

I tried again, but with no better success. Then my match went out. I made one more desperate jab in the darkness, and by good luck, out came the card!

There was not a second to be lost in examination of the card I had retrieved. I bounded down the stone steps, vaulted the courtyard railing, and ran to where I had left the messenger-boy's machine. As I swung it around I could still see the red light, distant and faint, getting ominously smaller.

Giving the machine a run forward, I threw my leg across the saddle. The spark caught promptly, and I was off again, triumphant. Although several blocks in the rear of the taxi, it was plain enough sailing. I opened up the throttle and heedlessly violated every speed law of the District. It was well for my purpose that the street we were in was not one with traffic blocks.

The taxi turned eastward along Massachusetts Avenue, and by that time I was sufficiently close to dismiss all present thought of being shaken off. Cab and pursuer went at a good pace along the smooth asphalt pavement.

After several blocks we arrived in a busier section of the city, where there were many persons on the streets, and I realized for the first time that a man in evening dress and a top hat must cut an extraordinary figure on a motorcycle. I could see people stopping on the sidewalk to stare at me. Some of them called out as I went by. To invite pursuit was the last thing in the world I desired.

It flashed upon me, too, that already there might be a police alarm for a motorcycle stolen by a thief in full dress. I promptly tossed my silk hat into the street and buttoned my overcoat across my shirt bosom. After that I seemed to attract little or no attention.

As we entered a less select section I began to wonder which way my exquisite woman of mystery was heading. Her taxi maintained its even pace, however, and there was nothing to do but follow the easy trail.

A few moments more and the white lights of a broad plaza came into view, and I realized we were making for the Union Station. That gave me a shock of surprise, but I had no time to reflect as to whither I was going. That was a matter entirely in the hands of my quarry.

The taxi ran in under the carriage entrance at the west end of the big terminal building, while I stopped at the corner outside. I saw her alight, pay her driver, and enter the station. Leaving the motorcycle propped against the curb, I ran toward the door through which she had disappeared.

"Here!" I said to the carriage starter, who was frankly surprised at my hatless state. "There's a motorcycle out there. Telephone the Western Union people that a machine belonging to one of their boys is at the station."

I handed him a bill and dashed away in pursuit of Mary without awaiting the answer.

Half-way across the waiting-room I sighted a vivid shimmer of silver, and knew I was still unbeaten. She did not stop at the ticket windows, but went steadily ahead toward the doors that lead to the train concourse, walking at a rapid pace.

"In for a railroad journey," I muttered. "Where to?"

I felt in my pockets and found, fortunately, that I had some money left. When she disappeared through a doorway I was forced to run, for I did not propose to lose sight of her. She was just handing a ticket to a gateman as I reached the concourse. Then, to my dismay, I saw the gate begin to swing shut.

A shout attracted the gateman's attention, and he held the gate open for me as I ran.

"Ticket!" he said sharply, as I attempted to brush past him.

"I've got a book," I answered, as I pushed my way through.

I heard him growling something about regulations, but he made no further attempt to stop me. The silver cloak was some twenty yards ahead of me, and I followed, prepared to step behind one of the pillars that upheld the shed if she should chance to look behind her.

The train conductor was calling "All aboard!" and she quickened her pace to a run. I followed her example. A brakeman assisted her up the steps of a day coach, and I swung aboard at the same spot just as the train started.

On the platform I paused cautiously, for I did not propose yet to let her know I was following. I could see her going down the aisle until she neared the forward end of the car, where she took a vacant seat and began staring out of the window. There were not many passengers. I seated myself near the rear door on the same side of the car. In front of me were two men, and I figured it would be easy for me to conceal myself behind them in case she happened to turn her head.

Not until I was settled in my seat did it dawn upon me that I had not the slightest idea where we were going. I had not even looked at the sign-board in the station, so ardent had been my anxiety not to be left behind.

Presently the conductor entered the car and came slowly along the aisle, taking up some tickets and punching others. Hers he collected. When he reached me I proffered him a five-dollar bill.

"Where to?" he inquired.

"Where are you going?" I asked.

He stared at me for a few seconds, observed a hatless man in evening dress, and evidently concluded I was not a friend of Volstead.

"This is a New York express," he said.

"Where's our first stop?"

"Baltimore."

"Take out to Baltimore, for the present," I said.

He subjected me to another scrutiny, but made change without comment and handed me a conductor's receipt. I huddled down in my seat, so that my eyes were just on a level with the top of the seat ahead, where I could comfortably watch the big white fox collar on the silver coat without much danger of detection.

I attempted to make a logical review of the situation, but found the task quite beyond me. The rapid succession of events had driven logic out of my mind. Only two things seemed fairly clear to me. The first was that my lady could not be journeying far in a day coach at this hour of the night, garbed in elaborate evening apparel and unaccompanied by any baggage.

The second was that she was not, after all, a detective. The mere matter of her meeting acquaintances at the White House settled that, so far as I was concerned. Everything that had happened since the moment we entered the White House was so utterly at variance with the theory that she was a professional sleuth I could no longer entertain it. Yet why had she undertaken the task set her by the tall man? And who was he? And who—to consider a far more bewildering problem—was she?

As the train rolled northward, she gazed steadily through the window at the midnight landscape. I soon ceased to fear the possibility of her discovering me; her attitude indicated she was completely absorbed with her thoughts. As we entered the cut which signaled the nearness of the Baltimore station, she straightened up in her seat and began fastening her coat about her throat. Then I knew we had reached another step in our journey.

The train drew slowly in at the station platform, and I waited until she passed out by the forward door. I rose quickly from my place and slipped out on the rear platform. I allowed her a fair start up the staircase that led to the street level, and followed, being careful not to let her get beyond view.

She did not enter the waiting room proper, but walked directly toward the taxis, entered one, gave a direction to the driver, and closed the door. I waited till the machine had started, then hastened forward and entered one of my own.

"Follow that taxi," I said to the chauffeur. "Don't let it get more than a block away, and don't get any nearer."

He nodded, grinning, and we started. I do not know Baltimore as I know Washington, and most of the streets through which we passed were unfamiliar. I could see through the front glass that separated me from my driver that he was not only vigilant, but cautious. He was faithfully following my lady's chariot, yet not so closely as to run the risk of attracting attention.

Not until we reached a stretch of smooth macadamed road that led through a park, passing a reservoir, and turned into suburban roads did I succeed in locating myself. Then it came to me that the beautifully parked thoroughfare through which we had passed was Eutaw

Place. We had passed rows of great old-fashioned houses for a considerable period, and I was wondering just how far our journey would extend when we turned off toward the suburbs. So we were not to stop in town at all. Where in the world were we headed?

For about a mile further we went, my taxi-man using his wits to keep the car ahead from suspecting he was following. When it seemed we were due for a real trip in the country, I saw my lady's car slow down and halt. She stepped out and seemed to be paying her driver—a surmise confirmed a moment later when her taxi started off and left her beneath the big trees in front of a gate. I immediately left my own cab and handed the taxi-man his fare, with a reward for his success.

"Want me to wait?" he asked.

"No," I answered.

He was not out of sight when I was sorry. Here I was, deposited somewhere out in the country, at a lonely hour, upon what might most likely prove to be a fool's errand, dressed in no costume for night strolling, and minus a hat. More than likely I would need that taxi, after quickly convincing myself that my pursuit, for the present, was at an end. But it was too late to indulge in these speculations; my conveyance was far down the road.

The girl had passed through the gate, up the wide brick walk, and was ascending the low porch. I moved forward, keeping close in the shadow of the big trees beside the vine-covered brick wall. At a safe distance from the gate I paused. Her silver coat, glimmering in the moonlight, made her figure easy to discern.

She wasted no time here ringing a doorbell. She evidently had a key, for in a few seconds I saw her disappear into the darkness of the hallway and caught the click of the latch as the door closed behind her. I stepped forward rapidly, and did not halt until I was beside the gate through which she had entered. At first I could not see a single light in any of the front windows of the house; but as I stood watching there was a faint glimmer at the edges of closely drawn shades on the lower floor.

The house was a Colonial one of red brick, and stood two stories high, with a low basement. It was broader than it was high. The whole exterior was exceedingly plain, but it gave an air of quiet, roomy comfort. It was a quite isolated estate, as if its owners cared much for their privacy, for on one side there was not a dwelling in sight, the last one we had passed being hidden by a slight rise in the ground, and on the other side the nearest neighbor, I judged, was a good half mile away, my judgment being by the faint glimmer of light I caught through the trees at a distance.

I did not dare risk going in through the gate, so retreated a short distance and vaulted the low brick wall, stepped across the lawn diagonally and walked along one side of the house. I had noted that the brick wall in front of the estate ran along its front to a considerable distance beside the road on each side of the road,—how far I could not judge in the moonlight.

But I was surprised to discover as I reached the rear of the house that the same brick wall, considerably higher—ten feet in height at least—enclosed the entire living quarters of the estate. At least I could discern the outlines of it on two sides, and I was curious enough to want to know if the wall was also at the back. I walked a long distance, two city blocks, I should judge, before I came to the rear wall I had expected would be there. Truly, the owners of the estate were exclusive.

The ground I traversed was laid out in two sections, divided by another brick path. On one side were the vegetable and flower gardens, and arbor and berry vines; on the other merely a plain smooth stretch of closely cropped, well-kept lawn. It came to me that the owners probably had this in reserve for tennis courts or something of the sort.

Retracing my steps, I made an inspection of the other side of the house. It was much the same as the other, with the brick wall in front losing itself in the blackness, and the side wall merely discernible as shadow. I returned to the road, again vaulting the vine-covered front wall at a distance from the house.

Here, for the first time, I took note of the tall windows on the lower floor of the house and saw they were gridironed by heavy bars. Burglar protection, I supposed, though why necessary so far from town I could not imagine; yet they gave a prisonlike air to the place that was not lost upon me. The light was still burning in the lower front room. The windows above were as dark as before.

Well, here I was. I had the bird caged. What next? I had not the least idea.

I stood leaning against a tree, studying the somber dwelling. Then I roused myself, walked boldly to the front gate, through it, up the walk and made for the front door. I had no definite plan; I was guided simply by the thought that, having brought my quarry successfully to bay, it would be a faint-hearted act to abandon the hunt.

I found a heavy knocker on the wide front door, lifted it and let it fall resoundingly. I heard its reverberations. I waited. One minute—two minutes —passed, and there was no sound from the door-latch. I pounded the knocker again, and waited a patient interval. Still there was no response, though the sound went loudly through the night. The light still showed at the edges of the lower windows. I descended the porch and stepped back a few paces, to glance upward. There was no light above. I pounded the knocker for the third time, lifting and letting it fall several times, with short pauses between.

Presently the cautious raising of a window attracted my attention, and a glance told me it was on the lower floor; but the light in the front room had been extinguished.

"Who is it?"

I knew the voice in a moment. It was tremulous now, though.

"Nobody but I," I answered.

She knew my voice, too, for there was an exclamation of astonishment and dismay.

"You—you followed me!" she said, after a pause.

I stepped forward and peered at the window, but could not see her figure in the dimness.

"Of course," I answered.

"What do you want?"

"An explanation."

Silence, and then her low-pitched voice said:

"Go away—please! I beg of you! You—you don't understand."

"I certainly do not," I answered promptly. "That's why I came."

"But I cannot tell you anything. Will you go away?"

"No."

"To do me an everlasting favor will you go away?"

"I'm tired of doing you favors," I answered roughly.

Again silence; then the window-sash descended—which I took to be a signal our conversation was at an end.

At times I am stubborn. Now, I was not merely stubborn, but angry. I was resolved to see the thing through to some more definite conclusion than this.

I went back to the door and resumed my pounding with the knocker. I kept it up for ten minutes, perhaps, bringing no response whatever. I sat down on the top step of the porch, propped my back against a column, and lighted a cigar. I would stay there, I decided, until I had further speech with her, or until somebody came out and threw me over the brick wall into the road. The night was clear and mild. I was quite comfortable.

Perhaps half an hour elapsed when I heard the window softly raised again.

"Please go away!"

"Oh, no," I answered cheerfully.

"What are you going to do?"

"Sit here till daylight, if necessary."

"I dare not let you in." Her voice quivered.

"Then I'll stay out," I answered. "It's quite restful here."

There was a stifled exclamation of helplessness. I was glad I could not see my lady's eyes. They were her weapons. She might have vanquished me with those, but they were hidden in the darkness of the window.

"But somebody—may come," her voice faltered.

"Then I'll have company."

"Please—please go, Mr.—Mr.——"

"Mansfield," I supplied promptly. "You know the name."

There was another half-smothered exclamation.

"You say I know it?" she whispered.

"Certainly. I'm your man, you know. You were to make my acquaintance, if you recollect. You were to locate something, and he was to attend to the rest. Have you forgotten that?"

A sharp, low cry came through the window, followed by a gasp and a moment of silence. Then, tremblingly:

"How did you know that—how could you? I—I—"

"Let me in and I'll tell you how I know," I answered.

"I dare not!"

"I don't think you're carrying out your bargain with the tall man," I observed.

"That's—that's what I'm afraid of!" Her words were accompanied by something that sounded like a sob.

"Then I advise you to let me in."

There was another pause, and the window was slowly closed.

Certainly, the conduct of my lady mystified me beyond measure. I could make nothing of it. Yet I was more determined than ever not to abandon my quest of an explanation. I had settled back against the pillar when I heard the slipping of a bolt behind me and the rattle of a chain.

I arose as the door opened slowly, and saw there was a light in the hall.

"If you won't go, come in," she whispered. "Hurry!"

I stepped across the threshold and the great door closed behind me. She shot the bolt and adjusted the chain.

I turned to look at her. She was leaning back against the hall wall, one hand clasped at her throat. Her silver evening coat had been thrown aside, and she was again the slender white-gowned figure of the

White House. Only the figure was drooping, and weary and pitiful. And her eyes! There was terror in them. I have seen the same look in the eyes of a frightened deer, and it has never failed to arouse quick compassion in me.

"Don't be frightened, Mary," I said gently. "I'm not going to hurt you. We're just going to have a friendly talk."

CHAPTER V

THE illumination in the high-ceiled hall was dim, but through a heavy pair of curtains that hung across a doorway leading to what apparently was the living room on the right, I could see a bright light. I pushed aside the hangings, and by a gesture invited her to enter. She roused herself with an effort, and, her head bowed, preceded me into the room.

It was a large place, more than half the width of the house and fully forty feet in depth. It was not, as I had supposed, a living room, but a library. Every available bit of the wall space had been covered to a height of six feet from the floor with shelves. How many thousand volumes they held I could not judge, but there seemed to be no vacant places.

Everything about the room bore the look of age—the books, the chairs, the great center table, the few paintings that adorned the somber walls, even the curtains. It looked like the habitation of a recluse. There was a pipe organ at the farther end of the room, an old-fashioned affair, dingy and dusty. On the floor was a heavy, soft, old rug. Some dead logs lay in a wide fireplace, and white, feathery wood ashes were scattered about the hearth. Everything conveyed a suggestion of neglect.

She walked slowly to a big, deep chair drawn up to the table, sat down wearily, and looked up at me. Her silver coat, thrown across the davenport in front of the fireplace, was the only bit of lighting in the otherwise drab picture.

I saw I was expected to say something, yet now I had cornered her I found it difficult to begin. My mind was wholly occupied with the curious picture of misery she presented.

"The time has come to be perfectly frank with each other," I remarked finally.

She made an almost involuntary gesture that implied neither assent nor dissent.

"Don't you think so?" I asked.

She shrugged her shoulders and made no answer.

"Perhaps I'd better begin by asking questions, if that will make it easier for you."

"How did you follow me?" she burst out suddenly.

"That's quite a long story," I replied. "I'll tell you later, but it's not material now. Let me ask, first, whose house is this?"

She hesitated, then answered:

"Mine."

Mechanically I glanced around the musty library. It did not look like a woman's house.

"And who are you?" I asked.

"Is that necessary?"

"I think so. At least, your name is Mary?"

She nodded.

"Are you Mrs. Vinton?"

"No!" The sudden vehemence of her reply surprised me.

"But you remember, at the White House—"

"That was all a lie. I couldn't help it."

"Yet the ladies received announcement cards," I said wonderingly.

"I know; but it was all a lie."

She nervously twisted a lace handkerchief between her fingers and avoided my eyes. I had remained standing, but now I drew a chair forward and sat opposite her.

"Then your name is Mary Donaldson?"

"Yes."

"And you are not married?"

She shook her head slowly and murmured a faint "No."

"You live here in this place—alone?"

"Yes, I live here for the present," she replied, watching me.

"There are servants here, I presume?"

"No."

I paused in astonishment, trying to grasp the fact that this dainty, almost fragile creature occupied in utter loneliness such a great and dismal place, so far in the country.

"You know my name is Daniel Mansfield," I next observed.

"Yes; I know it."

"What else do you know about me?"

"Very little, I think." She spoke hesitantly.

"Simply what the tall man told you, I suppose?"

She assented with a nod.

"And what is his business with me?"

"I—I cannot tell you. You must not ask me."

"Why?"

"Because I dare not tell you. He would—"

She caught her breath sharply, and the filmy handkerchief parted in her fingers.

"You fear him?"

"Yes!" It was a whisper, and she looked suddenly toward the door and inclined her head as if listening.

"Are you expecting him?" I asked, taking the cue from her action.

"No; not now."

"Are you in his employ?"

"No-o."

"I took you for a detective at first," I said. "Are you?"

She shook her head mechanically and asked quickly:

"How can you possibly know about—about—"

"About the orders you received at the Capitol?" I supplied. "That's simple. You and he were standing on one of the whispering stones, I on another. I heard nearly all of the conversation."

"He doesn't suspect it, I am sure," she said, after she understood.

"Probably not; it was a mere accident. Now, who is this man?"

She waited so long without replying that I added:

"Is he Vinton?"

There was a reluctant confirmatory nod of her small head.

"The man to whom you are supposed—by some of your friends, at least—to be married?"

"Yes."

"His name is Robert Vinton, I suppose. Who is he?"

"I—I must not tell you. I am afraid. Oh, please don't ask me, Mr. Mansfield!"

"I'm sorry, but I must ask you. What concern has Mr. Vinton with me?"

"I don't dare to tell you. If you knew him, you would understand."

"But you must admit, Miss Donaldson, that I am fairly entitled to know something about this business. Something apparently concerns me closely. I hear a woman receive orders to follow me, to discover something. I see her obey. I am led by her through a most extraordinary afternoon and evening. Then I am abruptly cast aside in a fashion as inexplicable as any of the events that preceded it. Naturally, I am led to believe in some sort of a plot against me, if I may call it that. Now, what is the plot, and why?"

While speaking, I had mechanically thrust a hand into the pocket of my vest, and my fingers came in contact with a bit of pasteboard. I drew it out and glanced at it. Until that moment I had completely forgotten the incident of the card under the door.

She leaned forward, as if suddenly possessed with an idea, and spoke rapidly.

"Will it be sufficient if you know that I shall take no further part in the matter, Mr. Mansfield? Will you let me go and try to forget it ever happened? I admit I have done wrong. I am much ashamed. I—I really am not what you probably think I am. I just did it because I was forced to; I did not dare refuse. But when I left you at the White House I had given it up. Truly I had!"

"That doesn't explain anything to me," I countered, avoiding her eyes. I knew, without looking, they were appealing to me; I did not propose to succumb again. "If this man Vinton tells you to go ahead, what will you do?"

She made no reply.

"You'll take his orders as you did before," I concluded harshly.

Again I glanced at the card I held in my hand.

"No, no!" she protested. "I'll abandon it all. I promise you!"

"Then how about this?" I asked.

The card I handed her bore the simple engraved words:

MISS DONALDSON

On the reverse side had been written with a pencil:

Cannot get information to-night. Still working.

She looked at the card in dumb wonder as she recognized it, then at me. There were both amazement and fear in her face.

"How—how did you get this card?" she faltered.

"I found it under the door where you left it."

"You saw me? You were there—in Sixteenth street?"

"I could give you a complete history of your movements from the moment you left me at the White House," I answered. "Perhaps I'm a better detective than you."

She was breathing rapidly, and her face had paled.

"That doesn't quite sound as if you had abandoned the matter," I urged. "Now does it?"

"That was another lie—what I wrote on the card," she answered faintly.

"How am I to know that? You take Vinton's orders when he gives them, even though you don't appear to like them. Suppose he tells you to continue—you will, of course!"

"No, no!" She nervously tapped her satin slipper on the thick rug.

"You tell me 'no.' Will you say the same thing to Vinton?"

"Oh, I don't know what to do!" she moaned, bringing her hands together with a convulsive gesture, and interlocking her fingers. "But I won't follow you again; truly I won't."

"Then why did you write on the card 'still working'?"

"It was to gain time," she said quickly. "It was to make him think I had not given up. I dared not tell him I had. It was just to gain a few hours' relief."

I began to believe she had told me the truth concerning her motive for writing the message, but I was not at all convinced the tall man would not set her on the track again. That she was in terror of him was plain in every word and action.

Suddenly she rose to her feet with a quickly drawn breath, and glanced in the direction of the door. The card seemed to fascinate her eyes.

"You must go away—at once!" she exclaimed.

"But there are several things I have not learned yet, Miss Donaldson."

"Go—please! He will be here!"

"Vinton?"

"Yes."

"I thought you said you were not expecting him."

"I wasn't. But the card! Oh, why did you take it?"

"Because I felt it concerned me."

"When he finds no message he will come here," she cried. "It was to keep him away that I left it. He was expecting it. That was the arrangement. Now he will be here!"

"I am sorry if his visit will be an annoyance to you," I said. "But I shall be very glad of the opportunity to have a little talk with Mr. Vinton."

She stared at me in horror.

"You must not meet!" she cried. "You—you do not know him!"

"But I have a desire to, Miss Donaldson. And the way seems to have been paved."

She stepped toward me swiftly, grasped my arm in her slender fingers, and almost dragged me to my feet with a strength that astonished me.

"For Heaven's sake, go!" she cried. "You cannot, you must not meet—here!"

"It seems as good a place as any," I answered carelessly.

"Must I get on my knees to you?" she pleaded. "I tell you he is dangerous!"

I smiled at her. I am not naturally timid, and, up to a reasonable point, I am big enough to take care of myself. The mere size of Vinton did not appal me. During the war I had seen many a Boche as big or bigger than he.

"Mr. Vinton is not going to hurt me," I answered confidently. "Besides, if he is in the mood you apparently fear, it probably will be better for me to stay on your account."

"That would only make it worse—afterward!" she exclaimed. "He must not know you have been here. He will believe I have played false. And then—then—" She broke off with a sob.

"I'll explain how I got here," I soothed.

"Will you go?"

"But you forget my own interest in the matter."

"Somebody may be with him, too!" Her agitation was increasing every moment.

There were several reasons why I did not propose to go. I wished to meet this man. I was determined to find out why he was having me watched. Again—and this was by no means the least of my reasons—I shrank from the idea of leaving the girl to face single-handed, in a lonely country house, a man of whom she was in pitiful fear.

"I don't mind if he brings a complete body-guard," I told her, boastfully.

"I'll meet you—to-morrow," she said, desperately, "if you'll only go!"

I shook my head stubbornly.

"I'll go only on one condition," I said. She waited expectantly for me to go on. "That you tell me the real reason, so far as you know it, why Vinton is having me followed, and what he wants with me."

"And if I tell you, you will go? You promise?"

I nodded. I did not tell her how far I would go, for I was resolved to watch the place from the outside.

"Then listen," she said hurriedly. "Mr. Vinton has learned that you—"

She stopped suddenly and listened.

"Somebody is coming!" she whispered. "It's he!"

Her quick ear had caught the purr of a smooth-motored car in the road outside, of footsteps on the brick walk; but I heard nothing until I heard the grate of a key in the outer door.

"Whoever it is cannot get in until you open the door," I said reassuringly. "The chain—"

"But I must let him in! Hide—oh, quickly! Upstairs!"

"But I tell you I wish to meet him!" I protested.

Both of us could hear an impatient rattling of the protecting chain on the front door.

"For Heaven's sake!" she pleaded, impulsively placing her hands on my shoulders and looking at me in abject terror.

The brown eyes won again. I stepped swiftly toward the portières that screened the hall, prepared to make a dash upstairs; but it was too late.

The door was pushed in a couple of inches, while the man rattled at the chain. I saw the girl go forward, heard her fumbling at the chain. The interval was long enough to enable me to run swiftly toward the rear of the library, the soft rug making my footsteps practically noiseless.

There was a pair of heavy sliding doors at the end of the room, evidently leading into another room; but before I reached them, I caught sight of another door that seemed to lead into the hall, thus making a second entrance to the library. Then the hall door swung wide, somebody entered, and I heard the door close again.

My hand was on the knob of the door that opened to the rear part of the hall. I turned it softly and opened up a crack of two or three inches. That end of the long hall was in comparative gloom. Putting my eye close to the crack, I could see the figure of the tall man standing under the light. I could not see the girl, but I imagined she was on the threshold of the library. He was removing his coat in a leisurely fashion, after which he turned and tossed it carelessly on the old-fashioned hall-stand. His hat followed it. He sauntered into the library.

As he entered the room I quietly vacated it, at the other end, and stood breathless in the hall. I did not dare close the door behind me, but left it as it stood, half open. The hall, however, was no place for concealment; it was a mere makeshift.

"Upstairs," she had told me. Evidently that was a place Vinton was unlikely to visit. I resolved to make a try for it; but to do so it was necessary to reach the foot of the staircase, and that was opposite the main entrance to the library.

I heard the creaking of a piece of furniture, and gathered from it he had seated his huge bulk in one of the chairs. Up to that time no word had been spoken. I tiptoed carefully along the hall toward the staircase. As I neared the portières he said sharply:

"Who has been smoking?"

I held my breath. Through some luck, the burned-out end of the cigar I had been smoking, though, was still in my hand. I had not made the mistake of tossing it into the fireplace.

"Why, I have, of course," I heard her answer.

The steadiness of her voice astonished me. Then I could hear him sniffing.

"It smells like a cigar," was his next remark.

"I haven't taken to that yet," said the girl, pertly. "It was a cigarette."

He laughed shortly.

"Have you any objection to my cigarettes?" she asked, a little belligerent.

"Not the least." There was a faint irony in his voice. "Only—" he was sniffing—"only it smells like a cigar."

I had been stealing softly forward during the colloquy, and was at the edge of the curtains. Inch by inch I leaned forward till I caught a glimpse of the girl's figure. She was standing with her back toward the portières, close to them, and one hand had drawn them partly together. Her intent was plain. It was to give me a chance to make the stairs.

Stooping low, I swung around the newel post, and went swiftly up the heavily padded stairs, as old-fashioned as the rest of the house furnishings I had so far seen. I placed my feet close to the wall and the banisters, so as to avoid any creaking of the treads; but near the top there was a dry old board that groaned in spite of me.

"What's that?" I heard him exclaim quickly.

"It sounded like something creaking," her cool voice answered. "The old place is always doing that."

I was at the head of the staircase by this time, completely screened by the gloom of the upper hall, and I turned just in time to see his tall figure step out from the library.

He glanced first at the front door, then down the

hall in the opposite direction, and last up the staircase. His head was bent forward in an attitude of close attention. For nearly a minute he stood thus, listening. Once or twice he sniffed, and I knew he was still suspicious because of the cigar smoke.

At last, however, he seemed to be satisfied, for he turned quietly and reëntered the library. I rested my elbows on the banisters in the upper hall and leaned over.

"Report, please," I heard him say in an even voice, "and in detail."

CHAPTER VI

HER answer to his command, which was cold and incisive, I could not catch. I leaned farther over the rail and craned my head downward. His next remark indicated that her reply had been unsatisfactory.

"Must I cross-examine you in detail?" he asked. "Have you spoken to him at all?"

"Yes." I caught the word faintly.

"Did he tell you where it was?"

"No."

"Did you ask him?"

Her voice dropped so low it was inaudible, but I knew the nature of her answer from his next words.

"You never asked him, then? Why not? Didn't I give you sufficiently plain instructions? Come, out with the whole business! It will save time, and I haven't any to waste."

"There was really no opportunity," she replied.

I heard him utter an exclamation of impatience.

"What are you doing with that gown on?" he asked suddenly. "Did you go to the White House?"

"Yes."

"With him?"

"Yes."

"And still you say you got no results. Why not?"

"I met him in the afternoon," she said slowly. "I did what you told me to; but there was no way of bringing up the matter. So I put it off until the evening, thinking there might be a chance then. I had the invitations, you know, so I asked him to go with me."

"He was easy, I expect." Vinton's voice had a sneering tone.

"He was willing to go," she went on steadily.

"And you were willing to go with him," he broke in. "You wouldn't go with me. All right! Go ahead."

"There isn't anything more to say," she answered. "I simply could not get the information."

"What was the matter? Were you afraid?"

"We were interrupted too often. We met some people."

"People you knew?"

"Yes."

"And you passed him off for me?"

Her reply was inaudible, but it brought a short, unpleasant laugh from him.

"A good joke," he said. "Then what happened?"

"Why, we left the White House, and I said goodnight to him."

"And you mean to tell me that was all you accomplished? Spent an afternoon and evening with this gentleman and bade him good-night, without even an attempt to obey instructions?"

"I tell you there was no opportunity. He would have become suspicious."

"Sure you're not playing double with me? Does he know who you are, or why you met him?"

Again her reply was lost.

"You were to leave a message for me," he went on. "Why didn't you?"

"You mean at Purvis's house?"

I made a mental note of the name. Somebody named Purvis lived in the darkened house on Sixteenth street, where I had stolen Miss Donaldson's card from under the front door.

"Certainly at Purvis's. There was no message."

"But I left one," she said. "I went there and rang the bell, and nobody answered. Then I wrote it on a card and placed it under the door. Did you look in the vestibule?"

"Yes, and found nothing."

"But I wrote it on one of my own cards. I said I could not get the information to-night."

He uttered an exclamation of disgust.

"It would have saved me a trip if I had found it. What time were you at the house?"

"It was a little after eleven, I think."

"Well, why didn't you wait? Purvis and I were in before twelve."

"I wanted to get the train. It was late, and I was alone."

"And now what are your plans?"

There was a moment of silence, and then I could hear her say, in a tone that seemed to imply a sudden firmness in her:

"I want you to release me."

"Release you? From what?"

"From going any further in the matter. I cannot— I cannot!"

"The deuce you can't!" he said easily. "You will have to keep on with it."

"I cannot do it, I tell you. I'm not fitted for it. It's humiliating; you have no right to ask me to do it. Get somebody else."

"I don't have to get anybody else while I have you," he remarked with such confident insolence I felt my anger rising.

"But I tell you it's impossible—for me. And—and he's not so easy, perhaps, as you think."

"How so?"

"He is already suspicious."

"Indeed! May I ask why? Did you give him some reason?"

"No; but I could see all the time he was waiting for me to say something. He never asked me any questions about myself. He seemed to—I can't express it exactly—seemed to sense the fact that the initiative belonged to me."

"And you, as usual, lacked initiative." He sneered at her.

"If I lack it, who is to blame?" she cried out with sudden fierceness. "You have made it your one object

—yes, ever since I knew you—to make my will subservient to yours. You have frightened me, threatened me, taught me to believe I have no self-reliance; that I must lean upon you, obey your orders, be your servant, even to the point of degradation. If I have no initiative, it is you who have robbed me of it; you have mocked me, and terrified me, and broken me!"

The sentence ended in a sob.

"We'll not argue it," he responded lightly when she had finished her outburst. "We'll grant it. We'll just get to the point of what you're going to do next."

"Nothing!"

"Oh, yes. You're going right on with the job. Look at me!"

The last words were spoken with such sharpness I was startled.

"Look at me!"

Half a minute of silence followed. I began to pity the girl downstairs; I could picture a silent ordeal that was the quintessence of refined cruelty.

"I see you have concluded to go on with the matter," he said finally, with a grim chuckle.

"I—I don't know. Don't look at me that way!"

"I know, however. You made an appointment with him for to-morrow, I suppose?"

"Yes—but I'm frightened. Please, Robert!"

She was lying about the appointment. She had fled from me without even an explanation. I began now to realize the grip of terror this man apparently had upon her. She was lying to save herself.

"Where is it?"

"In the Capitol again."

"All right! I'll be there to see; and this time there'll be no failure on your part. Do you understand?"

"Yes." The reply was so faint I barely caught it.

"What time is this appointment?"

"Eleven o'clock."

"Well, you'll know what I want to know by three. Don't forget that."

"But—but that's so little time," she protested weakly. "Give me more time. It may not be possible—"

"A whole day has been wasted already," he interrupted. "Purvis is complaining. He was nasty tonight because there was no word from you. That's what brought me out here."

So Purvis was in the thing, too! Who was Purvis? I could not recall anybody of the name. Purvis, of Sixteenth street! I knew where he lived, at least; it ought not to be difficult to get some particulars concerning the gentleman.

"I don't see why you got into it at all," she said. "Why was it necessary?"

"That's my affair entirely. It is sufficient for you that I have agreed to help Purvis. Besides, Lazare is impatient, and is talking about taking other measures. He may throw us both down."

Lazare! That was another new one. At least, I was getting names, even if an explanation were still missing.

"I wish to Heaven he would!" she cried vehemently.

"Naturally. But I don't propose to give him an excuse. I've told Purvis it can be done, and it's going to be done. There's a guarantee if we deliver; and a big guarantee if it's a success."

"Money! Money!" she cried. "That's all your life—money! You drag me into this just for money."

"A man has a right to expect something from his wife," he remarked with placid coldness.

"I'm not your wife!"

"It's practically the same. You soon will be."

"You lie!"

Her low voice was almost shrill as she flung the words at him. I could hear him quietly laughing at her.

"The cards are out, if you will recollect. Not invitation cards—announcements."

"Your work!"

"Certainly, and excellently done. And you admitted it this very evening at the White House."

"I—I—"

"If you were going to deny it at all, why didn't you deny it then? At the very first opportunity you acknowledged it. Do you wish to know why you didn't deny it? I will tell you. You lacked the courage. Perhaps you had a little courage once; I don't know. I'm not particularly interested. You have none now—none! Do you hear me? Whatever you may have had is mine. Look at me and tell me you have courage. Well, why don't you? Look at me!"

He paused and gave her a full opportunity to answer. If she said anything, I was unable to hear the words.

"Not having the courage," he resumed smoothly, "you will continue to admit to other persons that you are my wife, until the situation logically results in the formality of a ceremony."

"I would rather die than that!"

"Oh, no; I think not. You're not old enough to die yet. And you haven't the courage for that, either. I'll admit you're stubborn; I haven't been able to get all that out of you yet—but I will. Be sure of that! It's not so important, anyhow, because stubbornness without courage is merely negative. You're just a negation at present. The reason you'll marry me is because you still have pride and shame, and a particularly keen sensitiveness to the opinions of others. I don't mind your having those things, not at all. They're a help—to me. When I got your courage away from you I took the first and biggest step."

His voice was cool, even pleasant, which made the words he was saying to her a thousandfold more shocking to me than if he had spoken them roughly or in passion. He seemed to have an instinct for inflicting exquisite torture and a delight in watching the effects of it. I could imagine her, white-faced and with terror-stricken eyes, helpless against him.

"It isn't that I want you particularly," he went on. "You're all right in your way; you're good looking and well enough bred, and all that sort of thing. But I'm not infatuated with you at all. I just need you. You are useful to me. You are quite docile now; you'll be even more so after a while. But you won't mind that. I shan't be cruel to you, if that's what you're afraid of. Not in the least. So long as you're careful to obey me, there'll never be any friction at all. And you will obey; that's settled!"

Apparently Vinton had refined his method to the uttermost point. It was like the steady, even dropping of water upon a stone. Reiteration was his maxim. It was only a question of time when the stronger will could dominate completely; when she would come to believe—yes, to know—that what he told her was the truth, and that her courage was gone.

Yet I think even he was surprised at the sudden fury which was now aroused in her. Perhaps, had she known she was alone with the man, there would have been no outburst; but she knew I must be listening, and every ounce of pride and mortification in her leaped to her own defense. She was being made a pitiful, contemptible creature—within my hearing. It was not hard for me to understand the revolt, but I imagine it puzzled Vinton.

"I will not obey!" she said in low, trembling tones. "I will not marry you! I will endure all disgrace, all humiliation before that. I do not fear you. You think you have taken my courage from me. You lie! You are loathsome—contemptible—brutal. You have attempted the most horrible torture a man can inflict upon a woman—to make me lose my own good opinion

of myself; to make me pity and despise myself. And
I tell you I will not!"

She was defending herself, not to Vinton, but to
me.

"And this is the end of it!" she went on rapidly, her
voice rising slightly. "Do you hear? The end of it!
I don't care what comes—what people may think.   I
am tired of lying and deceiving and playing the slave to
you! Why should I keep it up? Just for you? Because I have been weak, do you think I shall always be
so? For your sake? For the sake of an unspeak-
able—"

I could hear him get out of his chair with a swift
movement. The sentence died on the girl's lips, or
rather ended in a gasp of terror.

"Stop!" she cried.

I whirled around the curve in the banisters and
started down the staircase, heedless of any noise I
might make. My blood was leaping, my brain afire
with rage. My own affair had vanished completely
from my mind. I was intent only upon averting murder—yes, murder, for I believed Vinton was easily
equal to it.

Half-way down the stairs, I paused, catching sight of
his tall, almost gaunt figure. His back was toward me
and he was standing quietly, his hands at his sides, his
head bent forward, looking down at her.

Less than half a dozen feet separated them as she
faced him. She was meeting his eyes steadily enough,
but there was an uncertain twitching at the corners of

her mouth. Vinton, of course, saw it. He was at the business of conquering her with one of his looks. More merciful would it have been had he taken her by the throat and choked her life out there and then! But that was not the way of the tall man.

I stood fascinated, watching them. Presently her eyelids fluttered and her erect figure began to droop. The tense hands slowly relaxed. At last her glance left him. Vinton took a step forward, but still his long arms hung loosely at his sides. As he moved, she shrank involuntarily.

I descended another step, ready to make a dash for him if he moved so much as a foot closer to her. I remember, also, that even in the excitement of the moment I resolved to shout as I closed in on him, in order to halt him before he reached her.

She saw me on the staircase. Our eyes met for only an instant. She glanced back at Vinton, who was still standing motionless and watching her. She was irresolute for a few seconds, like some baffled and tortured creature. Then she slowly bowed her head; it was like an act of submission.

With a dry laugh Vinton turned away from her and walked toward the rear of the library, passing out of my view. She looked up in a flash as he did so, caught my glance, and made a frantic gesture for me to go back. I waited long enough to see her resume her drooping pose of defeat, and carefully retraced my steps to the head of the staircase.

The last thing she wanted, evidently, was an encounter between Vinton and myself, or even a meeting. Rather than that, she was willing to yield to anything, or pretend to yield, at least. Yet I think—even though she appeared to submit to the man's will—that she took some courage from the fact that I stood ready in her defense.

For a couple of minutes there was nothing said in the library below, and then his voice broke the silence, speaking calmly:

"Apart from all other reasons, one thing which will make it necessary for you to marry me is the will. Did you forget that?"

She did not answer, and he went on:

"Unless you marry me, that will can never be probated. And you are quite anxious to have it probated, if I mistake not. You will not stand very long in the way of that. So, taking the developments in the case up to this point, and the fact of the will, and the further fact that you will do exactly as I say, I think we have a fairly good argument in behalf of a matrimonial alliance. Would it not seem so to you?"

Still there was no reply from her.

"So to get to the main point again," he said, with sudden briskness, "you will meet him again to-morrow, and will lose no time in finding out what Purvis and I and Lazare want to know. No further excuses will be accepted. Do you understand your orders? Repeat them!"

I could hear her voice murmuring faintly, and judged she was repeating his words.

"Very good," he added quietly.   "Now, where is that small satchel I left here?"

"I'll get it for you," she said quickly.

"I asked where it was."

"Upstairs, I think."

"I'll get it."

His figure appeared in the lower hall and he started up the staircase.   She was close behind him and halted him by laying a hand on his arm.

"I can find it easier than you," she said.   "Let me go up."

She was not looking at him, however.   Her gaze was directed upward, trying to pierce the darkness which hid me.   All the fear had come back into her face.

"I could not think of troubling you," he replied with ironical courtesy.

Having already mounted two steps, he resumed his journey upward on the third.   She fell back a pace and clutched at the curtains for support.

Two courses were open to me.   I must either meet this man in the darkness, or find a place of concealment—and the latter quickly.   My rage against him was sufficient to spur me into a meeting, although by the build of him I judged he would make quick work of me in a hand-to-hand fight.   But I thought of her and her agonized fear that he might find me in the house, and chose the second course.

He was nearly half-way up the stairs when I shrank back from the head of the steps and began to grope my way rapidly along the wall of the upper hall, which was in total darkness. My hand fell upon a doorframe, and then upon the knob of the door itself. I turned it softly, and the door yielded.

Thanks to the thick rugs with which the whole house seemed to be fitted, I could move without any perceptible noise. Pushing the door open sufficiently to make a space for my body, I squeezed through and pushed it to after me as far as I dared. I did not risk latching it, for Vinton was too close.

What sort of a room I was in I had not the least idea. It was pitch-black within. Very carefully, with one hand thrust behind me as a fender against obstacles, I backed away from the door. Half a dozen paces, and my hand came in contact with a desk or table. I felt along the edge of it, and then made my way around it until it was between me and the door.

As I ran a hand over its surface, I became aware of the presence of books and papers, and at last I encountered something heavy, which proved to be an inkstand. I grasped this firmly in my hand, lifted it from the table and waited.

Vinton pushed open the door.

The light from the lower hall cast a faint reflection against the wall beyond the staircase, not enough to illuminate the upper corridor, but sufficient to enable me to discern the towering figure silhouetted against it. He stood on the threshold, took one step into the room and appeared to be groping for something. I drew in my breath slowly and held it.

I could hear his hand sweeping along the wall and a mutter of impatience that came from him. I realized he was feeling for the electric switch, probably the usual pair of push buttons set in a metal plate beside the doorway. The house I had already noted was well fitted for electric lighting, though so far from the city. If Vinton pushed the button, well—

I lifted the heavy inkstand and drew it back. Not the slightest compunction about what I should do entered my mind. I was going to let him have it the instant the lights went up.

The button clicked. The room remained in darkness. Vinton muttered an oath.

In a flash I realized what had happened. Whoever had left the room last had turned off the lights at the bulbs.

He made a step forward, as if entering in search of one of the lights. I held my heavy improvised weapon ready, resolved to let fly in the darkness if he came too close.

"I think it's in the front room!"

The words floated up from below, sharp and clear. Whether she divined the situation or not, I had no means of knowing, but it seemed as if a sixth sense had prompted her. She may have guessed I had retreated into the nearest room.

The sound of her voice brought Vinton to a stop. He turned slowly and groped his way back to the door.

"Why didn't you say so in the first place?" he called

down to her as he stepped back into the hall and groped his way along to the front of the house.

I exhaled my breath softly and set the ink-stand back upon the table, but did not let go of it. I heard him turning the knob of a door, and a glow of light in the upper hall signaled that he had found an electric switch in another room.

He was in there for about a minute; but the light went out, and he came back down the hall. He paused at the doorway of the room where I was hidden; then he went on to the head of the stairs and descended slowly.

"Did you find your bag?" I heard her ask.

"No," he answered shortly. "It doesn't matter for the present. I've no time to waste on it."

There was a sound of more low conversation in the hall below me. Then the front door opened and closed, though I heard no accompanying rattle of the chain, and there was stillness in the house.

CHAPTER VII

I WAITED a little while, listening, to make sure he had gone, and began groping about the table to see if there was a light. My hand finally found what proved to be an electric drop-light, and with a pull of a chain I had the place illuminated.

The room in which I had sought concealment from the tall man was large, although not more than half the size of the great library downstairs. At first I took it to be an improvised office of some sort, but as I viewed it further it seemed to be a curiously incongruous combination of office, study, museum and laboratory. It was not at all like a woman's room. So interested did I become in an inspection of it I did not think of Vinton, and forgot my own feeling of shame at having played what seemed a pusillanimous rôle during the last half-hour.

The table was a businesslike piece of office furniture. Upon it were a large writing-pad, a number of books, a basket for letters at one end, and a cabinet of three small drawers whose markings indicated they contained a card-index. At one side of the table was a typewriter stand with a machine upon it; at the other a dictaphone.

One end of the room, that nearer the door, was entirely covered with shelves enclosed in glass cases. They contained a mineral collection and innumerable small pieces of pottery and carved images, some of the latter strangely grotesque. Another set of shelves ran along another side of the room—the side that formed part of the outer wall of the house—their continuity being broken only by a large fireplace, set with andirons, but bereft of any logs or signs of a recent fire.

One section of those shelves was entirely given over to dictaphone cylinders. There were literally thousands of them, grouped into subdivisions marked with letters and numbers. I judged the card-index related to them, and that they were kept as records of some sort. It seemed an odd fashion in which to preserve records.

Out of curiosity I took one of the cylinders from a shelf, slipped it into the dictaphone, turned the switch and placed the receivers to my ears. The voice was that of a man, by the accent evidently a fellow countryman; but the words were French, a language I do not understand. I replaced the cylinder on the shelf after listening a few moments, and resumed my tour of the room.

The shelves beyond the fireplace contained a motley collection of electrical apparatus, tools, a few books on chemistry, more minerals, some stuffed birds, several trays of old coins, a jumble of various kinds of metallic ore, arranged without apparent order, nautical instruments, including a collection of compasses which contained specimens I had never seen before, plaster statuettes, miniature models of boats, and dozens of other objects of which I knew not the use, and which seemed to be arranged without order or discrimination. The disarray of this part of the room was in sharp contrast to the precision with which the collection of dictaphone records was grouped and indexed.

The farther end of the room, next to the windows, which I imagined opened upon that great stretch of gardens and smooth lawn I had earlier traversed, was given up to a chemical laboratory. On the opposite side was a work-bench, with an electrically operated lathe and a fine outfit of instruments for working in metals.

I wandered back to the table and picked up a leather-bound volume that bore the outward appearance of a ledger. It was not a record of accounts, however, but apparently contained the results of a series of chemical experiments. There were many mathematical calculations on its pages and some words I could not recognize, although all the written matter was in French.

I suddenly remembered the girl downstairs, whose presence in the house the strange conglomeration of the room had for the time completely driven from my mind. I went out into the hall and called:

"Miss Donaldson!"

There was no reply, and I repeated the call in a louder tone. Still no answer.

As I went down the stairs I noted that Vinton's hat and coat were gone from the stand. Mary was not in the hall. When I reached the foot of the staircase I stepped into the library, that room being still lighted.

She was not in the library. I stood looking about me in blank fashion, then walked slowly down the length of the big room, thinking perhaps she had collapsed in a faint, following the ordeal through which she had passed, and might be lying concealed from me by some of the bulky pieces of furniture. But there was no sign of her.

Again I looked into the hall, and went down to the rear end of it. The search revealed no trace of her.

Retracing my steps to the front door which I noted was not chained, I opened it. After listening cautiously, I went out onto the porch. There was not a living thing in sight. The nicely-tuned car in which Vinton had arrived had gone with as little noise as it had come. The road in front of the brick wall, with its rows of heavy shade trees, was as still as a tomb.

Mystified, I went back into the house, closing the door behind me. I listened, but could hear no sound save that of my own breathing. The girl had vanished. Was it possible that, after all the bitter controversy between them, she had gone with Vinton? I recalled then that there had been a short final conversation between them in the hall, spoken in such low tones I could not hear the words. Perhaps, in that last minute, Vinton had changed the whole plan of action, and had forced her to go with him.

Back into the library I went, and there I was convinced she had left the house. Her silver brocade coat, which had been thrown across the davenport in front of the fireplace, was missing, an incident I had overlooked when I had first searched the room for her. Mary had eluded me again.

I sat down and tried to figure the thing out, but could make no sense or logic of it. I wondered what the sudden change of program signified. I could not feel that she would leave a stranger to roam through the great, solitary mansion she had told me was hers. I could only conclude that Vinton had peremptorily taken her away with him, she not daring to hint to him I was in the house, and there being no way she could notify me of her departure.

I was free, apparently, to inspect my lady's domicile at my leisure. It might only satisfy idle curiosity; yet there was also a chance it would throw some light upon the strange business which seemed to revolve about me as an axis. I concluded to have a look at things.

The first thing I did was to try the sliding doors that led to the room in the rear of the library. They were locked and there was no key. At the end of the hall another door led to the same room, but this was also fastened. I did not feel that my privilege as an un-invited guest extended to the breaking of locks—at least not yet—so I turned my explorations elsewhere.

Another door in the rear of the hallway led into a wing apparently flanked in the rear by the vegetable, fruit and flower gardens. There was little of interest there; a dining room fitted in the period of another day as was the library and hall, and beyond it a room that had evidently been given over to the servants as a sitting room. Behind them came a pantry, kitchen and store room.

Leading from a small hallway that connected pantry and kitchen with dining room was a stairway leading to the cellar, and down this I went in pitch darkness, stepping carefully until I reached the bottom. Conveniently I had some matches in my pocket, and I struck one. Within close reach of my hand was an electric fixture and I switched it on.

I was in a partitioned-off cellar with a concrete floor and deep as the basement of a city dwelling. But my tour here, as well, added nothing to the value of my information. It was the typical cellar of an old-fashioned country house. There were more store rooms, swinging and other shelves for fruit and vegetables, and an electric-driven motor for pumping water, near the tall boiler in which water was heated by the kerosene heater beneath it. Apparently, while not too far from the city for electricity, the owners of the place must depend on other means than municipal aid for water pressure.

There was also a furnace room, with a dingy old hot-air apparatus in it, and a pile of coal in one corner. The furnace was cold. The back of the cellar terminated in a heavy door which was chained and guarded with three wooden bars. It was also locked and the key was missing, so I made no attempt to open it. Evidently it merely opened into one of those paved areaways leading into a rear yard.

The most modern thing about the whole place was its

system of electric lighting. Fixtures had been placed freely and without regard to the amount of current that might be consumed. It was quite easy to get about.

I turned out the lights as I proceeded and went back up the stairs to the main floor. I stopped in the pantry, conscious of the fact that I was hungry. There was a considerable quantity of potted stuff and home-made preserves on the shelves, but I did not bother to open any of it, contenting myself with a box of crackers I found, and which I carried along with me as I returned to the main hall.

I was too curious to be much affected by the lone-liness of the place, although a strange and untenanted dwelling as somber as this one is not the most cheerful abode that can be conceived. Making another tour of the library, munching my crackers as I went, I crossed the hall and went up to the second floor. A door di-rectly opposite the head of the stairs opened into a bathroom, of which a brief inspection satisfied my curiosity. Since seeing the electric water pump in the cellar I had known it would be there.

I went forward through the hall, past the open door of the office or laboratory, which I had left illuminated, and came to another open door on my left, evidently the entrance to the room into which the tall man had gone. I felt along the wall and found the electric switch. This was a bedroom, but so prodigious in size its oc-cupant, whoever he or she may have been, must have had the sensations of sleeping in some vast public hall.

The most curious thing about it was the manner in which an old-fashioned four-poster, with a canopy, was placed. It stood, not against one of the walls, but in the center of the room, the head placed toward the windows at the front. There was a good deal of furniture in the place, most of it mahogany of an old and excellent type, including a particularly fine highboy. I opened both the closets in the room and found them hung with masculine garments, all of which were seedy in appearance and completely obsolete in the matter of style. Clearly, this was not the tall man's wardrobe.

There was a smaller bedroom at the forward end of the hall, but it was plainly furnished and quite uninteresting, save for an oil painting that was hung there. The subject was a woman, dressed in the garb of half a century ago. I did not think much of it as a work of art, but something in the face puzzled me. It did not occur to me what this was until I had left the room, and I went back for another look.

Beyond doubt it was a portrait of an ancestor of my lady—perhaps her mother. The resemblance to Mary was unmistakable, particularly in the great brown eyes that looked out from the canvas. There was no name on the picture. I could not even find the artist's signature.

Remained now the rooms over the dining wing and I lost no time in opening the door near the bathroom which apparently led to them. It opened into a smaller hall running at right angles to the big main

hall. Here the rooms on the side of the hall at the
rear of the house were smaller and bore a deserted look.
I gathered they had been occupied—those in the rear—
by the servants; but now nothing but a few simple
articles of furniture remained in them.

There was a larger room in front, however, which
was evidently in present use. A glance into one of its
closets revealed the familiar pleated brown dress, tan
hat and mink coat my lady had worn when first we met.
Yet there was no air of permanent occupancy about the
place; it conveyed the impression it was merely being
used as a sort of temporary camp.

A dresser contained a few toilet articles, including
a small silver tray on which were several pieces of
jewelry. One of these was an old-style wedding ring,
which I idly examined. The single word "Mary" was
engraved on its inner circumference.

"Perhaps her mother's, or her grandmother's," I
thought.

This was the only place in which I felt myself an
intruder, and I withdrew after a brief inspection.
When I returned to the main hall and reëntered the
office, or study, or whatever its owner chose to call it,
I found that, absent-mindedly, I had carried away the
plain gold ring. Making a mental memorandum to return it to its place before I left the house, I dropped
it into my pocket, and sat down in the big chair which
faced the desk.

My tour of inspection had taught me little, so far
as throwing any light upon the interest of Vinton and

Mary in my own affairs. In fact, I had learned nothing at all. And who were Purvis and Lazare?

As I sat staring in front of me, pondering in a confused way over the events of the day and night, my eyes fell upon an object on one of the lower shelves, which at first awakened no curiosity in me, but which, as I studied it idly, suddenly made me sit forward with a start. It was a small bag.

Vinton had spoken of such a bag; it had been the object of his uncompleted search. Was this it? I lost no time in speculation, but quickly crossed the room and brought it over to the table.

I discovered it was locked, but a metal paper-cutter proved to be an effective instrument for forcing the flimsy fastening. There were some papers inside, and I emptied them out upon the table. The first I picked up was an envelope addressed to "Robert Vinton," and I knew I had fallen upon the tall man's property. The address was one of the well-known hotels in Washington.

There was nothing of importance in the letter which this envelope contained; at least, nothing important to me. It was from a business house in New York, and concerned some trivial purchase. There were several other letters of a similar character, two or three railroad time-tables, and a recent bulletin issued by the Patent Office.

I found another letter addressed to Vinton in a sprawling, masculine hand. It bore no stamp or postmark, but had evidently been carried to Vinton's hotel by messenger. It was brief, but there was enough in it to startle me, and to throw a sudden flood of light upon certain events. It said:

Lazare getting impatient, and so am I. Must obtain quick results or his clients will make other arrangements. Must have demonstration within ten days. Urge all haste in learning where Mansfield compass is located, so further steps can be taken. Keep in touch with me.

PURVIS.

Now that the thing was set out before me, I wondered why I had never thought of this explanation before. My aëroplane compass was the object of all this sleuthing and mystery and hocus-pocus!

The compass was one of two things which had kept me in Washington for the past several months, the other being Jeanette Fenwick. Of late, Jeanette had almost put the compass out of my head, although it was that which had taken me to the capital in an effort to interest the government in its possibilities.

Professionally, I am a civil engineer; in an amateur way I am an inventor. Ever since the war, I had been interested in aëroplanes, for, during the war, I had belonged to a flying squadron, but only, I am forced to admit, as a sort of extra to fall back on in case of dire need. My training had been sketchy, and I never would have been overseas had I not joined up so early in the game, and before all the daring university men got in. After that there had never come opportunity for my limited services, and my training had been left incomplete. I had known little of handling the stick myself, though I had made many flights as second man in the machine.

But, as an also-ran member of that flying squadron, I had had opportunity to recognize both the value of aëroplanes and their short-comings, even with the rapid strides they had made. I had thought of my compass a good deal, but the principle of the thing had not come to me until quite suddenly one day, after I had been reading a naval officer's report on the limitations imposed on the use of aëroplanes as fleet auxiliaries because of the need of a completely satisfactory instrument to enable the aviator invariably to locate his own ship, after it had passed beyond the range of his vision, or should the radio fail, or the plane get outside the radius of its radio apparatus. There seemed to be just some little thing lacking in all the compasses so far in use.

I say the principle of the thing came quickly to me; but it took many months of patient labor to develop a device that would carry out that principle. And then, rusty as I was, in the years since the war, and with the great difference in planes now and then, it took me, even after I had solved my problem, a few more months to again become a capable enough pilot to enable me to make my own tests.

I went to Washington, satisfied I had something no nation could fail to seize upon. It meant, if my compass worked—and with my own eyes I had seen it work—that all the air-scouting squadrons of other countries would be inferior to those of the United States, because ours could navigate unerringly in fog, darkness, or over an unmarked sea.

I found what many another inventor had discovered before me—that the government is slow, cautious, always skeptical, even where anything it acknowledges the need of is concerned.

The army and navy were "interested"; the government might eventually buy. But there was much red tape and delay, much rigmarole of which I became impatient.

Meantime, I met Jeanette. Courtship, for the time, triumphed over compass. Jeanette occupied more of my thoughts than the government as a prospective customer. The slowness with which my business proceeded through official channels was an invitation to neglect it, and I did.

So this was the explanation of Vinton, of Mary, of Purvis and Lazare—my aëro compass!

I sat staring at the brief letter, much in the same dazed frame of mind as a man suddenly awakened from a dream. Well, why hadn't they come to me about it? I had no contract with the government. I could sell anywhere I chose. Naturally, being an American, I preferred selling it at home.

Who wanted it? A government? I supposed so. The letter spoke of Lazare's "clients." That might mean a government or it might not, but I could think of no interest that would be so deeply concerned in a matter of this kind as a government with a big military mind. Why all this underhand, mysterious business of doing things by the indirect route?

How long I should have remained sitting like a statue, wondering over this revelation, I have not the least idea; but I was suddenly brought out of my reflective mood by a noise downstairs. It sounded like the cautious opening of a door.

I bounded out of my chair, thrust Purvis's letter into my pocket, and sprang toward the hall in such haste I knocked over the stand which carried the dictaphone, so that that instrument fell to the floor with a crash. As I reached the hall I heard the noise again, this time as if a door had been quickly closed.

Half-way down the stairs I paused and listened, but now the house was as still as death itself. The front door was closed.

I completed the descent and ran into the library. Not a thing there had been disturbed. The big doors that led into the room beyond were still closed and locked; so was the door that entered it from the hall. Yet I was absolutely positive I had heard a door open and close on that floor.

I ran to the front door and opened it. No one was on the porch. Peering out into the night I saw the lawn and road beyond were as silent and deserted as when I had viewed them before. Returning inside, I slipped the chain on the door as well as locking it.

As I stood there in the hall, listening again, my

sensations were anything but pleasant. I am not timid, but I object to things I cannot understand.

Once more I made a tour of the library and tried the doors that led to the rear room, without result. At first I considered attempting to force one of them. I decided to wait a little longer and give this noise, whatever it was, a chance to repeat itself.

I went slowly back upstairs and resumed my seat in the office, after picking up the dictaphone and setting it to rights as best I could. It was nearly half-past one o'clock. I lighted a cigarette and waited.

Twenty minutes, perhaps, elapsed. Then I heard the noise again!

Surely it was the opening of a door. I knew I could not have been mistaken before. I rose noiselessly from my chair and tiptoed out into the upper hall, leaning over the banisters. From my vantage-point I saw a white figure moving slowly and hesitantly along the hall below, going in the direction of the front door. It was Mary!

Her silver coat was thrown over one arm, her bare shoulders were glistening white as she paused for an instant under the hall light. I thought for a second she was going out of the house. Then, with a helpless gesture, she turned and began to ascend the stairs.

I stepped back into the room and waited. She came up slowly, as if each step went to the limit of her physical endurance. When she came into view opposite the door, she paused and saw me standing there. There was not the least trace of surprise, resentment or anxiety in her face—only weariness.

"Won't you come in?" I said.

Without answer, she crossed the threshold, went over to the big chair by the desk, and sat down.

CHAPTER VIII

FULLY a minute she sat there, her eyes half closed, her figure relaxed, her hands hanging listlessly. I could see she was undergoing the effects of a sharp reaction, and I waited quietly for her to say something, although I was afire with impatience to ask her many questions.

At last she looked up, her great brown eyes staring at me dully, as if her mind were working very slowly.

"You would not go away!"

She said it helplessly, almost petulantly, accompanying her words with a limp gesture.

"No. I wouldn't go. Did you expect me to?"

"I wanted you to. What good can come of it?"

"You wanted to make me believe you had gone away with Vinton."

She nodded wearily.

"Why, Miss Donaldson?"

"I didn't want you to question me any more. I thought when you found me gone you would not wait. It seemed the easiest way to end it. And I'm so— tired."

"I suppose you know I overheard most of the conversation below?" I asked.

"That was one reason I wanted you to go," she answered slowly. "I didn't want to see you after that; it was so—so humiliating. I felt I could never face you."

"But I was ready to help you, if you needed help," I reminded her.

"I know; I saw you. Oh!" She buried her face in her hands. "Oh, he is a terrible man! He frightens me so. Sometimes I feel as if I should die when he looks at me. I can hardly breathe."

"Has he ever harmed you?" I asked gently.

"Physically, you mean? No, that is not his way. If he struck me down with his fist it would be infinitely kinder; but he strikes me with his eyes—and his tongue. He looks at me—oh, I can't tell you!"

"Hypnotizes you?" I suggested.

"No, not exactly that. He just terrifies me. And he keeps telling me I am nothing—just a mere pawn, a thing without initiative or will. And it's true! That's the bitterness and the horror of it; he has made it true."

Her glance roved wildly about, and finally rested upon the bag, which I had left lying on the table. She looked up at me inquiringly.

"It's Vinton's," I nodded. "It was on the shelf over there."

"And you've found out—"

"A little; yes. Enough to explain where I come in. Under the circumstances I took the liberty of examining its contents."

"Then you know what Vinton wants, and why I—"

She broke the sentence off abruptly, and I saw it was difficult for her to speak of what she had done.

"What I don't understand," I said, "is why Vinton is able to make you do something you don't want to do. You don't look like a woman whose mind is a mere piece of putty. I don't believe you are. And I don't believe that Vinton, without some sort of a lever to work with, could transform you into a mere machine without resolution or volition. Haven't you anybody who can help you?"

She hid her face again, and I heard a dry sob.

"No friends? No relatives to whom you can go?"

"It's too late," she whispereed. "Too late! And he's right—Vinton is right! I haven't any will, any courage. It's all gone—gone!"

"Nonsense!" I said sharply. "If you keep telling that to yourself, which is what he wants you to do, you'll believe it some day. But you don't believe it yet."

"Do you believe it?"

She looked at me as if fearfully awaiting a verdict.

"Certainly not. You're overwrought; you're pretty nearly on the edge of a break-down. But that's all. You say you've nobody to go to with your troubles?"

"Not here."

"Tell them to me, then," I said briskly. "Perhaps I can suggest something."

"Tell you my troubles—after what has happened?"

She stared at me incredulously.

"Why not? I'm mixed up in this thing, it appears. I may as well know more about it. The trouble with you is that you've had no one to talk to."

She nodded dumbly, her gaze fixed upon me as if trying to assure herself I was a friend rather than an enemy.

"You will despise me," she at length murmured.

"Oh, I'm sure I won't," I replied, assuming a cheerful tone. "Besides, I want to help, if I can."

"You really mean that?"

"Absolutely. We may be able to help each other."

She seemed to consider this; then she roused herself from her listless attitude and leaned forward in the chair, resting her elbows on her knees. I was sitting on the desk, swinging my feet, and looking down at her.

"Once upon a time—" I began suggestively, with a smile.

I was trying to divert her mind from what seemed to be the tragic side of things. There was an involuntary flicker of amusement in her eyes, which faded quickly; but I knew she appreciated my attempt.

"My people are in England," she said. "My father, my two sisters, my brother. I have no mother."

"That was her picture I saw in the smaller bedroom?" I interrupted.

"Yes; she has been dead for several years. My father is James Donaldson. He has lived abroad ever since my mother died. We were all with him until I came back on a visit last fall. I was born here and educated here. All my friends are here. I came to spend the winter."

She paused, as if trying to arrange events in sequence.

"After a little time in New York, I went West, to Los Angeles, where I have many friends. And Vinton followed."

"He's from the other side?" I asked.

"He's English. You wouldn't recognize it, I know. He has lived most of his life in the United States, and he's more like an American in his speech and his actions. But he was born in England. That's where we met him. He wanted to marry me over there."

"And you wouldn't?"

"How could I?" she asked in a surprised tone. "I don't love him."

"I see." I nodded gravely. "What then?"

"My father wanted me to marry him. I would do almost anything for my father, but I could not do that. You don't understand about Vinton. He can be anything he wants to be. You have seen only one side of him; he has many. He made a very strong, a very favorable impression upon my father. And his position in England is good; he knows excellent people. But, somehow, I never liked him. I didn't distrust him —then; yet I never really had confidence in him. I really made the trip to this country to be away from him. But he followed."

"All the way to Los Angeles?"

"Yes. Of course I had to introduce him to all my

friends. And they liked him and entertained him. He can make friends wonderfully, if he wishes. He has brains and education and manners; culture."

"Money, too?" I asked.

"No, I think not. He is supposed to have it, but I do not really believe he has. Else why—but I will come to that in a moment. While in the West I received word my father was very ill, and then, almost at the same time, a cablegram that he was dying. I was nearly frantic. It would have taken me eleven or twelve days, at the very least, to get home. I wanted to start at once, but Vinton persuaded me to wait for further news, urging that if my father was really dying I could not possibly reach him in time. And then there was another cablegram, and it said—"

Her voice broke.

"It said that my father's last hours would be happier if he could know I was Vinton's wife."

"And you—"

"What could I do?" she cried, throwing out her hands in an appealing gesture. "I worshiped my father, and now he was dying; and the message said I could make him happier. It was the last thing I could do for him; and yet—oh, I could not bring myself to do what he said!"

"Your friends in Los Angeles knew of his request?"

"No, I did not show them the last message. I was ashamed. They simply knew that he was ill. But Vinton knew it. He saw me reading it, and took it from my hands. He wanted to know what I would do. I told him—I had told him so before—that I did not love him, and that neither of us would ever be happy if we married. He was very kind and deferential about it; he told me he understood how I felt. But then, gradually—and oh, so cunningly!—he led up to what he said was the best solution. It was to cable to England I had married him, to soothe my father's last hours. He would not hold me to it, he said; he would still hope that I would gradually learn to care for him and really become his wife, but if I found it impossible he would not press the matter. I was so dazed I scarcely knew what to do; and that was the beginning of his control over me. I cabled my father a lie—I said I had married Vinton. Oh, was it wrong of me? I don't know; I was completely bewildered."

"It was a hard situation," I admitted, without attempting to answer her question.

"And then—" Once more she faltered. "Then, two days later, I received a cablegram that my father had passed the crisis."

"He is alive?" I exclaimed.

"He is nearly well," she answered. "And he thinks I am Vinton's wife!"

"You have never told him otherwise?"

"I dared not; I was ashamed. I was afraid, at first, that it might kill him; after that it was too late."

"And Vinton knew of this message you sent?"

"Of course; he suggested it. And then I began to

know the true Vinton. Never saying a word to me, he had announcement cards printed, and he sent them to all my friends in the East whose addresses he knew."

"And to your friends in Los Angeles?"

"Oh, no; he was too clever for that. They would have known it was a falsehood. But he sent them East and abroad. He wanted to put me in a position where I could not retreat without shame and humiliation; and he succeeded! It was after that he began to dominate me, to frighten me, to make me understand he had placed me in his power. I was afraid to send.word to my father that I had lied to him. Vinton told me that only one course remained—I must marry him or be forever disgraced. And he was right! He had me trapped. But I would not marry him—then. I evaded it. I had nobody to advise me. I was ashamed to tell my friends. So I came East, just to get away from him. I had no hope of escaping him always; but I wanted time. I went to Washington and hid in a hotel there for three days, without letting any one know I was in town. Then another thing happened; it seems as if everything has been tragedy of late. I read in a paper that my uncle—Rufus Jennings—was dying."

"This is his estate?" I asked quickly. I had read much of that particular Baltimore millionaire, whose eccentricities were much in the news.

"Yes. So I came to Baltimore; but he had died before I arrived. And then Vinton—he had followed me to Washington—read of it, knew where I must be, and followed me here."

"But where did Purvis come in—and Lazare?" I broke in.

"Vinton knew Purvis, it seems. I don't know just what he is; he lives in Washington and seems to be mixed up in government matters some way. Lazare is a foreigner, French, or Spanish, I do not really know. Vinton brought them here first; he made this place his headquarters. I could not help overhearing much of their talk. Gradually, I found out they were trying to get' hold of your compass."

"Yes, yes!" I exclaimed excitedly.

"I think it's a foreign government—a small one, rather—but I don't know which," she said. "Lazare is the agent. He went to Purvis, and Purvis enlisted Vinton. They talked a great deal about the money there was in it. They were trying to find out where the compass was; they knew it was somewhere in Washington, that you had been trying to interest the government in the matter. Vinton began to work on me. Steadily he had been trying to break down my will, to make me subservient to him. I was all alone in this place; even the servants left soon after my uncle's death. Vinton was staying in. Washington; he saw Purvis and Lazare every day. As I said, he often brought them here. And finally he compelled me to—you know what happened in the Capitol."

I nodded.

"Oh, I was ashamed!" she cried pitifully. "But I

was so afraid I did not dare disobey. By that time
Vinton was beginning to succeed; he had robbed me of
my courage. So I forgot I was a woman, and—
and—"

"I understand," I said soothingly. "You did the
only thing you could."

"But what did you think of me?"

"I didn't know what to think at first," I said frankly.
"But from the beginning I knew you were reluctant,
doing something against your will. Why, of course, I
didn't know."

"I ran away from you at the White House to-night,"
she went on, "partly because I knew I could never do
what Vinton wanted me to do, and partly because I
was ashamed to look you in the face after what happened there."

"I was going to ask you about that," I broke in.
"Mrs. McCutcheon—"

"Was one of the persons to whom Vinton sent wedding cards," she supplied. "It was she who, supposing
I was staying in my uncle's home near Baltimore, pro-
cured the White House invitation. I had not the least
idea of going; Vinton wanted me to go with him, an
additional grip on me; but I was stubborn about that.
When I failed to get to the point with you this afternoon, I was afraid to go back and tell Vinton so. I
thought of the White House, and I asked you to go,
thinking perhaps something might happen there which
would give me the information. But always I despised

the task, and loathed myself for being so weak! Can you believe that?"

"I do believe," I answered.

"When Mrs. McCutcheon met us, there wasn't anything else to do but pass you off as Vinton. I couldn't explain to her."

"And I helped to make the affair particularly difficult for you," I added.

She smiled faintly, but rather ruefully.

"What an amazing liar you must think I am!" she went on. "But I had to do it, after what you said. There was no other way."

"But Lieutenant Ferris?"

"There was a case, you see, of a friend who knew nothing of the supposed marriage. The moment he addressed me as 'Miss Donaldson' I knew that. It was a relief not to have to go through the same old lie for him."

"But you called me 'Mr. Larned,' if you remember."

"It was the first name that came into my head. I knew your name was Mansfield, but I couldn't think of it at the moment. Did it make any difference?"

"Only that Lieutenant Ferris addressed me by that name in the presence of Miss Fenwick."

"And she is—I had forgotten! I will not ask you to forgive me for that; but I will try—truly, I will—to explain the matter to her. If you'll let me know where to write, I will tell her exactly how it happened."

Her cheeks had taken on some color during the recital, which I could note, since what rouge she had

worn earlier had long since worn off and not been re-
newed. At this point they distinctly flushed. Gradually she had thrown off the despairing languor of the
last hour, revealing flashes of that animation which,
during the afternoon and evening, had astonished me
by reason of its contrast to her moods of almost gloomy
indecision.

Mary Donaldson, to reiterate, was a woman of no
common charms. As she leaned back in her chair, her
large soft eyes watching me doubtfully and timidly, her
bare arms and shoulders nearly as white as her gown,
the dark waves of her smart bob clinging closely to
her small head, her figure boyishly slender and girlishly
graceful, she was amazingly attractive—she compelled a tribute of the eyes. And, better than all else,
the terror-haunted look in her face had vanished.

"I think you had better leave the explaining of things
to me," I said, "so far as Miss Fenwick is concerned."

Why I smiled as I said it I do not know. I was
distinctly conscious of the fact it was likely to be an
unsmiling task, the explaining of that meeting—and
the earlier one of the afternoon—to Jeanette.

I told Mary how I had followed her from the White
House to Purvis's house, and how I had afterward
tracked her to Baltimore. She listened with the wonder of a child. It was simple enough; but there was
an element of adventure in it, of fortuitous chance, so
far as I was concerned, that stirred her imagination.

"There is something else I may as well tell you,"
she said, after a considerable pause. "You have heard

so much you may as well hear all. And it explains partly why Vinton is driving me. My uncle, Mr. Jennings, left a will."

"I remember that you asked me if I knew anything about wills,—this afternoon," I nodded.

"He was a curious man," she continued. "His wife died many years ago. They had one son. Uncle Rufus was not really a scientist, but he had an extraordinary smattering of things. This room must have puzzled you greatly. The smattering explains it. He dabbled in all sorts of researches, mostly chemical. I don't think anything he ever did was of value, in a scientific way; but he kept always at it. He lived here all alone, with his servants. If it had been left to Uncle Rufus to make his own living, he would have been a poor man; but he inherited his fortune, and he never wasted much of it. In late years I think it must have increased, because his personal tastes were so inexpensive. I was one of his favorites. We saw little of each other, yet he always remembered me, and frequently wrote to me."

"So you are your uncle's principal heir, I presume?"

"No, not the principal one—just one of them. He treated my two sisters and my brother exactly as he treated me. We are each to get one-fifth of his estate; the remaining fifth goes to his son, but it is left in such a manner that he can only obtain the income from it. My cousin is not to be trusted with money. He is useless and rather dissolute; not very worthy of anything. His father was quite well aware of this, and no doubt he thought it a kindness, rather than otherwise, to leave him an income only, so that he couldn't ruin himself with a fortune placed at his immediate disposal."

"I think I heard Vinton say something about the probating of the will," I said.

"Yes, it will never be probated, unless—"

"Unless?"

"Not until I marry him."

"But why?" I demanded.

"Because Vinton has the will!"

"You mean to say you turned it over to him?" I asked.

"No; he got hold of it. I couldn't help it. I told you how he made this place his headquarters. He took possession of it as though it were his. My cousin did not come home after my uncle's death, so Vinton and I made a search among my uncle's papers. It was he who found the will; and he put it in his pocket, after reading it aloud to me. So now he has another weapon."

Every moment, it seemed, I was getting more light upon Mr. Robert Vinton.

"And my uncle's will," she added, "also settles a part of the money allotted to myself and my sisters upon their husbands, if we marry."

"I see," I remarked. "Mr. Vinton seems to be a thrifty person, as well as—as several other things."

I sat on the table, swinging my legs and regarding her contemplatively. Whether she thought she divined something in my mind or not I cannot say, but she broke out suddenly:

"Please don't think I want the money. I don't. My father is not rich, but he has always had enough to care for us. Whether I ever get a cent from Uncle Rufus makes little difference to me; but don't you see what will happen if that will isn't probated. Everything my uncle had will go to his son—unconditionally. He is the only direct heir. If I refuse to marry Vinton, he will destroy the will. There is nothing but my word against his that such a will ever existed,—and he would deny it to the end. And if I allow him to destroy the will, I shall be the means of depriving my brother and my sisters of the money they are entitled to receive. Have I any right to do so?"

I shrugged my shoulders, not prepared to discuss the ethics of the problem.

"Vinton will carry out his threat; I know that. And not only shall I deprive others of a fortune, but I shall be the direct instrument of bestowing upon a worthless cousin a sum of money that will be nothing but a curse to him. So I must marry Vinton. I must!"

"Have you asked him to return the will to you?"

"He laughs at me," she answered hopelessly.

"But there must be some way to compel him—some legal process."

"Even if he shouldn't deny the existence of such a will, that involves the whole scandal and disgrace—the other matter. He knows I dare not proceed against him. He has two grips on me. Even without the will I should have to marry him."

"Of course, if you are determined to regard the thing only in the light of pride," I began, "why—"

"What else has a woman, after all?" she demanded quickly. "Pride is more than you think it is. It is the thing that keeps us up to our ideals. It is the thing which, after all else, will keep me from ever letting my father know I lied to him."

Her alternate moments of vehemence and depression I accounted for by the extraordinary strain to which she had been subjected in the last few weeks. That her natural spirit was high and independent I could easily believe; that Vinton had cruelly shaken, but not broken it, I was also convinced. Yet I was well satisfied he was in a fair way to complete his odious work.

"So you have resolved to let the will go to probate," I observed.

She leaned forward in her chair and regarded me fixedly.

"There is one thing that makes me hesitate about even that," she answered slowly, her low-toned voice tremulous.

"And that is—"

Often I found it necessary to supply a stimulating word, she hesitated so frequently.

"It is not my uncle's last will!"

CHAPTER IX

"YOU'VE found another will?" I asked breathlessly.

"That's just the trouble," she answered. "There is another, but I cannot find it."

"But how do you know it exists?"

She hesitated, as if to arrange certain facts in orderly fashion.

"Uncle Rufus died under peculiar circumstances," she said. "I told you I read of his last illness in a newspaper, and that when I reached here he was dead. He had some sort of heart trouble from which he had suffered a long time. During attacks, for hours at a time, he would be prostrated, while at other periods he seemed entirely well. The doctor who attended him during his last attack must have seen that it was bound to terminate fatally, but he did not realize that Uncle Rufus might rally sufficiently to leave his bed, even for a short time. Yet that is just what he did. On the afternoon he died, and less than an hour before his death, my uncle got out of his bed, put on a dressing gown, and went from the front room on this floor into the one we are now in. This was where he did all his work. There was, in the house, an old butler named Howard, who had been employed for a good many years by Uncle Rufus, and who was acting as his nurse. Howard had gone out of the bedroom for a few moments and did not know my uncle had got out of bed until after he came into the study.

"Howard was shocked when he returned to the bedroom and found Uncle Rufus gone. He ran into the study. As he entered the room, my uncle was slowly slipping from his chair to the floor. Howard ran and caught him, and, as he did so, he saw Uncle Rufus was trying to say something. He lifted him up in the chair and put his ear close to my uncle's lips. All he could hear was—'Another will—now.' And the next moment my uncle was dead."

She shuddered and rose from the chair involuntarily. It was the same in which Rufus Jennings had breathed his last.

"And that was all?" I asked.

"Just as he spoke, my uncle made a gesture with his hand, as if he was trying to point at something; but Howard was too excited to pay much attention to that. It's my belief Uncle Rufus was trying to indicate the place where the other will was kept, but his attempt was lost upon Howard."

"Have you made a search?"

She nodded. "Thorough."

"Downstairs?"

"No; it is somewhere in this room, if anywhere.

My uncle did all his work here, kept all his records here."

"But how do you know that the will Vinton has is not the one of which your uncle spoke?"

"Because it is dated nearly two years ago. And he said 'Another will—now.' Howard had seen the old will, and my uncle knew it. He would not have told Howard there was another one, therefore, unless he had made a new one. And when he said 'now' he seemed to mean, as far as we can interpret it, that it was of very recent date."

"Does Vinton know of this other will?"

"No. We kept it from him. We have spent hours trying to find it—Howard and myself; but it is of no use. It is not here."

"Where is Howard now?"

"He has gone back to his home in the city. Vinton would not let any of the servants remain after my uncle had been buried."

"He took charge of things?"

"Yes." She hid her face, then looked up. "I know it seems weak of me, but I have tried to give you an idea of what he can do."

I recalled the vivid demonstration that had taken place in the library not more than an hour before.

"So, if you don't find this other will," I began, "the one now in Vinton's possession will stand—"

"Will stand as the last one."

"Have you any reason to believe your Uncle Rufus contemplated any important changes in his will?"

"No. I didn't even know the contents of the first will until Vinton found it. But don't you see? No matter what the new will may contain, if it is the last one, then that which Vinton holds is worthless. And he loses that additional grip!"

She spoke eagerly, a new note in her voice. It was almost a note of hope.

"I can see you are still clinging to an idea you may not marry Vinton, after all," I said.

She looked at me with a flash of spirit, and shook her head.

"No," she answered slowly. "I can see no hope there. And yet—"

"But you do see it, even if subconsciously," I broke in. "Your manner says it, even if your lips do not. You are still hoping. You can't see the way, but you haven't given up. You've spent hours trying to find something that may weaken Vinton's grip. Why should you do that if you really thought a marriage to him was inevitable? You may not know it, but you're still fighting."

"Oh!" she cried, clasping her hands tightly to her chest. "I wish I could believe that!"

"Believe it, then, for it's true," I answered. "You've been falling into a bad habit of late, apparently—that of believing only what Vinton wants you to believe. You've been as weak as water, when you had no business to be weak. Vinton didn't obtain all his control over you at one stroke. He did it gradually. You let him do it!"

"But," she faltered, "there was nobody else—"

"There was always yourself," I exclaimed sharply. "For Heaven's sake, have you no self-reliance? No character? How old are you?"

"Twenty-three," she answered faintly.

"Twenty-three! And you've behaved like a child. I think I'd feel a little ashamed, if I were in your place."

"I—I am."

"Then shake it off! Be yourself again. You've got some character in your face, if I'm any judge. Why not live up to it? Do you suppose your father would want you to act as you've acted? I don't believe it. Why"—I was indignant, in spite of myself—"the whole business is utterly wrong—it's preposterous!"

She broke into a fit of sobbing. I'm a poor hand when a woman starts that. I wanted to run.

"You're—you're scolding me," she said miserably. "Just as—"

"There! Never mind," I interrupted in a gentler tone. "I didn't mean to scold. Only I was trying to show you that you're still possessed of your independence; that you're not somebody else's slave."

"If there was only somebody," she said. "Somebody else!"

"There is," I assured her. She looked up at me through her tears. "I'm here," I supplemented.

She seemed doubtful and incredulous as she stared at me.

"But how can you help?" she asked, wonderingly. "And why should you?"

"I don't know just how I can help—yet," I answered. "But I'm in on it. You see, I have an interest in the matter. It's Vinton. It looks as if he and I had some business together. I can't let things drop where they are."

"But I tried to help him against you," she said doubtfully.

"I'll not charge that up against you," I answered easily. "I'll balance it up with the information you've given me. Now, I'm not vindictive by nature, but I confess quite cheerfully I'd like to do Mr. Vinton a bad turn. I could do it with a very comfortable conscience. Tell me something—what was Vinton going to do, after he found out where my compass was?"

"I don't know," she replied frankly. "All I was to do was to learn where it was. He—they—never told me anything more than suited their purposes."

"Well, never mind. Now, as I understand it, the thing that would bother Mr. Vinton most, just at present, would be the finding of this other will made by your uncle."

She nodded.

"Then let's find it," I said, swinging down from my perch on the table.

"But we've looked—everywhere," she declared, although there was an expression of gratitude, almost of relief, in her face.

"We'll look again. You're reasonably sure it must be in this room, if anywhere?"

"Absolutely. My uncle kept nothing in the way of papers anywhere else. Only his books are downstairs."

"Did he have a safe?"

She shook her head.

"Let's go through the desk first," I said.

Between us, we made a systematic examination of Uncle Rufus's desk. We removed all the drawers from it and went over their contents with minute care. Most of the papers were written in French. It was his habit to keep his records in that language, she told me. He regarded it as the international language of science, and had the idea that he was about to bequeath something of infinite importance to the scientific world.

She read French with ease, and I submitted all the foreign-worded documents to her; but there was nothing among them that resembled a will. They dealt for the most part with experiments in chemistry, and I gathered from scraps she read to me that Uncle Rufus believed himself to be upon the trail of a new theory of protoplasmic life.

While I had no real hope that we should uncover a will, I concealed that from her, for the mere prosecution of a search seemed to instil energy and decision into her. For the time, she forgot Vinton. It was interesting to watch her, as she poked into age-yellowed envelopes, untied bundles of neatly folded documents, and delved through the pages of closely written manuscripts. She was alert, birdlike, animated.

I could not help noticing the pretty manner she had of using her hands; every movement she made was one of youthful grace. Her cheeks were glowing with the excitement and expectancy of a child fathoming a Christmas stocking. Sometimes she would strike a passage in French that amused her, and I would make her read it to me. Uncle Rufus never intended to be funny, but he had a quaint way of putting sentences now and then, a quaintness that seemed to be enhanced by translation, for more than once she and I laughed outright at the results of her efforts to render things into English.

If the desk concealed a will, it must have been in some secret drawer which neither of us could discover, for nothing in the papers we examined bore the least resemblance to a testimentary document.

From the desk we turned to the shelves, poking about underneath and behind the crazy conglomeration of odds and ends they contained, but finding nothing. We looked into chests of drawers, vases, boxes—anything in the nature of a receptacle—without result. We even disturbed the orderly arrangement of dictaphone records, and did not bother to reëstablish it; but there was no will.

I lifted the rugs, poked into the fireplace, sounded the walls, all to no purpose. Often, to what I thought would be the ruin of her white evening gown, she was on her knees beside me, peering into some corner that suggested a likely hiding-place, her head close to mine, her cropped dark curls lightly brushing my cheek, her hands touching my hands as we explored recesses where the eye could not reach.

We rummaged around like a pair of children in mischief. The task, to me, was a peculiarly pleasant one, made so by the mere presence of Mary Donaldson. Often I found my glance wandering from the search to her. The woman was more than attractive in those moments when she was her own mistress; she was appealing, alluring, compelling. And there was a quick energy about her that convinced me of the fact that Vinton had not broken her spirit, but only driven it into a refuge from which it emerged when the thought of him was absent from her mind.

Once she found me smiling and questioned me with her expressive eyes. I was holding in my hand a rusted spike which had been resting on a dusty shelf, and was reading the inscription on a paper tag attached to it. The words were:

Taken from a piece of wood supposed to have been one of the relics of the De Long expedition.

I read the words aloud to her.

"Wasn't it a tragedy?" she asked.

"I wasn't smiling at that," I answered. "I suppose I ought not to smile anyhow, but I couldn't help it."

"Tell me," she commanded.

"Do you remember the name of the ship in which De Long made his expedition?" I asked.

She shook her head.

"It was the *Jeanette.*"

"Still I don't quite understand you, Mr. Mansfield."

"Why, Jeanette happens to be Miss Fenwick's name," I replied.

"Miss Fenwick? Who—oh, I remember!"

She stood looking at me gravely, and then I caught a faint hint of amusement in her eyes.

"You find it suggestive of an arctic experience?" she asked softly.

"I'm afraid so," I answered ruefully, suddenly sobered.

Jeanette had not been in my thoughts for some time, but the memory of her last cold glance swept over me with disconcerting vividness. Mary was swift to interpret what she saw in my face, for she leaned forward and gently placed her hand on my arm.

"I'm truly sorry," she said impulsively. "I didn't mean to jest. But—but—well, you know you smiled yourself."

"I know," I nodded solemnly, putting the rusty spike back in its place.

When I glanced at her, her cheeks were slightly flushed and she was busily exploring a new prospect.

Jeanette! I vaguely wondered if Jeanette really had cause for anger against me, and whether she would accept me on the same old footing after she understood. I felt uneasy about it. There was something in the look she had given me that chilled me to a decidedly uncomfortable degree.

We said no more of my *fiancée,* but went on with what was becoming a more and more hopeless search. How long it would have lasted I do not know, if a sudden and startling interruption had not come.

Clearly and sharply the knocker on the front door clanged!

Mary drew her breath sharply, and, from her kneeling posture, sat back suddenly upon the floor, one hand raised to her throat.

Stupidly and mechanically, as if it were an act demanded by the occasion, I took out my watch and examined the dial. It was nearly three o'clock in the morning.

The knocker fell again, in a series comparable to dots and dashes, as if the knocker were impatient.

"Who is it?" I asked, rousing myself.

"I don't know," she whispered, her cheeks pale as chalk.

"Vinton?"

"I—I don't think so."

"I'll go and see," I said, rising from my knees.

She sprang up quickly and grasped me by the arm.

"No, no!" she cried. "It might be he, after all; and if it is, he must not find you!"

"We shall meet sooner or later," I replied, starting toward the door. "Why not now?"

But she dragged me back. The old terror was upon her.

"Wait!" she exclaimed. "Don't go yet!"

She dropped my arm, and ran swiftly out of the study and down the hall toward the large front bedroom. I followed as far as the doorway and heard the sound of a window softly raised. A few seconds later she was back again.

"It's some one with a big van," she whispered. "Out in the road."

"At this hour of the night?" I asked wonderingly. "Were you expecting one?"

"No."

The knocker was pounding, insistently, petulantly, even spookishly.

"Somebody has made a mistake," I said, starting downstairs. "We'll soon find out."

She followed me closely and huddled at my shoulder as I unchained the door, threw back the bolt and opened it. A bulky-looking young man was standing on the front porch. There was another figure out on the brick walk.

"Well?" I demanded.

His glance rested in surprise on the costume of the girl at my side, then he began searching a slip of paper he held in his hand.

"Lazare?" he asked finally, looking up.

Mary gave my arm a violent pinch.

"Yes," I said.

"Got a bunch of stuff out here," he went on. "Where do you want it?"

"This is a strange hour to be delivering goods," I said.

"Can't help it. Believe me, I ain't doin' it from choice. It's a special order. Ordered to deliver the stuff, night or day, as soon as it was dumped off the car, and it come in less than an hour ago. What'll I do with it?"

"Much of it?" I asked.

"Eight or ten cases," he answered grumblingly. "Some of 'em are long, too; and some of 'em are big— and heavy."

"You'd better take them to the garage," interrupted Mary. "You'll find the gate and the driveway a little further down the road. I suppose you'll be able to get them into an almost empty five-car garage. We'll go down and unlock the door."

We stepped across the threshold and started diagonally across the lawn as the man returned to his van and started his motor.

"We'll save time by not going by the brick path," said Mary, as she guided me toward the unseen garage. "The motor driveway has never been extended to the house. And there's only the station wagon and an old runabout in the garage now. Vinton is using the limousine for himself."

"So!" was the most illuminative comment of which I could think.

She unlocked the garage door with the key she produced from under a near-by stone as the motor van drew to a stop in front of it.

"You can carry them in this way," she said.

Standing together on the lawn, we watched the men

unload a series of boxes and crates from the van. They were of all sizes and shapes, including some peculiarly lengthy ones. Two of them, which attracted my attention particularly, were at least fifteen feet in length by six in width. It was with some difficulty that the two men juggled them from the van and to a resting place on the garage floor.

When the last of the cases had been stowed indoors, and I had signed "Lazare" in receipt for them, Mary and I stood looking at them in bewilderment.

"What is it?" I asked.

"I haven't the least idea."

"This stuff was shipped here without any notice to you?"

"Absolutely."

"Vinton and his friends seem to make pretty free with your place," I observed.

"Oh, yes," she replied, with a shrug of helplessness. "I expect anything of late."

The freight was all strongly put together. They were simply labeled "A. Lazare," with the address of the estate painted upon them in black letters, but no other inscription that would give the least clue to their contents.

"Mr. Lazare travels with a good deal of baggage," I remarked. "Show me where the tools are kept, and we'll get an explanation."

"No, don't," she said. "Leave them as they are. Somebody is sure to be here in the morning. It would be better not to disturb them."

Reluctantly, I acquiesced, and after closing and locking the garage doors, we went back to the house.

"Shall we have another look for that will?" I asked, as we entered the main hall.

"No, it's useless—I feel sure of that. What time is it?"

"After three."

"Oh, you must go. Please go now!"

In her sudden insistence and realization of the lateness of the hour, it escaped Mary that to obey her meant a pretty long walk along country roads for me before I could hope to reach transportation. But with a wry inward smile I remembered it.

"But we haven't settled anything," I protested. "What are you going to do to-morrow, for instance —or, rather, to-day? You told Vinton you had an appointment with me."

"Oh, I don't know. But you must go! Somebody might come at any time now."

"And leave you alone in this deserted place?"

"It will be daylight in less than an hour. I'm not afraid of that. Please go. Oh," she stopped suddenly. "I had forgotten. You have no car. Wait, I'll drive you—in the roadster—to the car line. Come!"

She snatched up a dark coat from the hall stand and jammed a small dark hat down over her dark waves. Before I realized it she had urged me through the front door which she slammed behind her and we were rushing across the lawn toward the garage.

"But I—I can't let you do this, Mary," I protested. "You'll have to return alone."

"If I'm not afraid of the house," she laughed, "why should I be afraid of the road. Nothing will happen to me."

In a businesslike way she got the car going, showing she was familiar with its mechanism, and as we whirled out through the still opened gate I was protesting:

"We can't let things go this way. I promised to help you, you know."

"There's nothing you can do," she answered. "Nothing!"

"But perhaps there is. In the first place, you're threatened with a relapse into timidity. I told you to stop that. I want you to keep your nerve. Take your courage in both hands and be a woman, Mary."

She straightened her slender figure that was bent over the wheel, turned her head slightly to look at me, and forced a faint smile.

"That's better," I said with a reassuring nod. "Now, listen. You don't want to marry Vinton, do you?"

"If I could only escape!" she murmured.

"You can."

I said it with an air of great confidence, though I had not much faith in my own words. I knew the brave front she was assuming would not last, once she faced the tall man again. She waited breathlessly for me to go on.

"If we'd found that second will, you'd feel a little more secure, wouldn't you?"

She nodded.

"And if Vinton hadn't got the other will, you'd feel still safer?"

"Yes." She said it slowly and hesitatingly.

"Well, we haven't found the last will, but we might get the other one."

"How?"

She glanced toward me, her eyes big with wonder and excitement.

"Why, I'll get it for you," I answered.

I did not have the shadow of a plan in my mind, but I made my words as boastful as those of a boy, principally for the purpose of infusing courage into her.

"You?" she whispered, incredulous.

"Certainly I will. Where does Vinton keep it?"

"I don't know," she faltered.

"Where does he live?"

She told me the name of the hotel, in Washington.

"I imagine he keeps it pretty close to him," I went on. "Anyhow, I'll find out."

"You mustn't try!" she exclaimed. "He is dangerous, I tell you."

"I'm tired of hearing that," I answered. "I'll believe he's dangerous when I get a demonstration."

I must confess that was sheer brag. In my own mind I was well satisfied Vinton was dangerous—

peculiarly dangerous; but I did not want the girl to know my thoughts.

"What are you going to do?" she asked quickly.

"Get the will," I repeated. "And I'll have an answer for you within the next few hours. You will be at home?"

"Yes."

Steering mechanically, her eyes were taking time to search my face wonderingly.

"I'll either report in person or get you a message," I said. "Meanwhile, stand pat. Don't worry. Don't make a move until you hear from me."

Mary nodded mechanically, as she brought the small car to a stop at the curb at the end of the trolley line.

"Good!" I said, as I swung open the door and leaped out. "And now, good-night—Mary!"

She reached over the door and gave me her hand impulsively. It was cold, but there was a firm pressure in her fingers.

"I thank you for what you are trying to do," she said simply.

"For what I will do," I corrected.

I stood looking at her, at the carven whiteness of her face under the street lights. Then I bowed my head, touched her fingers with my lips and turned toward the street car that was just coming to a rattling stop.

CHAPTER X.

THE hour on that early morning train from Baltimore to Washington was the first I had had in many for sober reflection. I was in evening dress, and hatless; but if anybody remarked my unusual appearance I was unconscious of the fact, for I was completely occupied with my thoughts. They were not, however, orderly thoughts.

Every little while a white figure would rise before me, obscuring my mental vision—the figure of a slender, dark-haired girl, who was now laughing and archly alluring, now fear-stricken and pathetic, now wondering and dismayed.

Save for this ever-recurring picture, my mind perversely drifted to trivialities. I speculated as to whether the messenger-boy had recovered his motorcycle. I recalled with a chuckle the expression of the clerk at the library, when we asked concerning Balboa. I laughed at the look of the indignant little foreign attaché who overheard my companion in the White House grounds, and reverted time and again to the conductor of whom I asked the destination of his train.

The really big things that had happened were evasive. Then, too, there was the persistent and distracting phantom of what seemed a great, rose-red lily, wreathed in the halo of a glowing beam of light. It seemed to sway before me bewilderingly, then slowly fade to white and disappear, only to return and glow with steadily deepening tints until it became again rose-red.

I must have dreamed some of it, for a reaction had come upon me and I was weary for sleep; but which was dream and which was the vision of a wakened mind I could not tell. I know, however, that in Washington, a brakeman had to shake my shoulder to arouse me.

It was six o'clock on a bright morning when I reached the capital, and twenty minutes later a taxi had carried me to my apartment. The first thing I did was to set my alarm-clock for seven-thirty. Then I undressed, took a hasty bath, and jumped into bed for an hour of rest.

This time I had a dreamless sleep. I remember lying stupidly for two or three minutes, listening to the recurring warnings of the alarm, before I realized a new day's work was awaiting me.

As I dressed, I found a sense of amazement at myself steadily growing within me. Chance had drawn me into a strange gamut of events; now, of my own volition, I was plunging farther into the unknown. Back there in the gloomy house nothing had seemed too extraordinary to fit the scene and the atmosphere; here, in my own quiet apartment, everything that had happened assumed a grotesque form and lost its reality.

What had I enlisted for? It seemed to me, as I looked at the business with a clear mind, that sufficient for me were my own affairs; but I had stepped out of them and taken upon me the affairs of others. Whither would they lead me? Having attained the age of thirty-five with reasonable steadiness and balance, was I about to embark upon an unfamiliar sea of adventure, of make-believe, even of arrant nonsense?

More than once I formed a resolve to drop the affair where it stood and wait for Vinton and his friends to make another move, if they so chose. But each time—and I was broad awake, too—would come the white vision, and I could see the great brown eyes appeal to me. The eyes conquered.

"Go to it, son," I said, half aloud, as I adjusted my scarf before the mirror. "You may be sorry, but go to it!"

Now that I was resolved to see more of the affair, and with my promise to Mary Donaldson ever recurrent in my mind, I found myself getting back on the mental plane of the night before. It did not seem to me astonishing, for instance, that before leaving my apartment I went to my desk, took out a small automatic, and slipped it into my pocket. At any other time I should have considered it insane to arm myself in this fashion.

As I ate breakfast in a near-by restaurant, I made an attempt to formulate a plan concerning Vinton. I had assured Mary with the utmost display of confidence

I would get the will for her in order to help break the hold he had upon her; although why I should happen to be so concerned in breaking that hold did not appear entirely clear to me. At any rate, I was to get the will.

But where was it? It was unlikely Vinton was foolish enough to carry the thing around in his pocket; he might have it locked away in a safe-deposit vault, for all I knew. All I knew was Vinton's address. Lacking a clue as to the whereabouts of this next-to-the-last testament of Rufus Jennings, the first logical step seemed to be in the direction of Vinton himself.

The walk to his hotel was not a long one, and it was not yet nine o'clock when I entered the lobby.

"Is Mr. Robert Vinton staying here?" I asked the clerk.

He consulted the room directory and nodded.

"I'd like to see him."

The clerk took up a desk telephone and called a number, and in a waiting interval asked for my name.

"Mr. Larned," I replied promptly, using the fictitious name she had given me at the White House.

I heard the clerk repeat it into the transmitter. He hung up the receiver and turned to me.

"Mr. Vinton says he does not know you, but if you care to wait in the lobby for ten minutes he will be down."

I nodded and strolled away from the desk. It was no part of such plan as I had to meet Vinton in the lobby, or any other public place. My business with him required a certain degree of privacy. I had learned from the clerk all I needed. I knew the number of Vinton's room.

Crossing the lobby, I stepped into one of the elevators and directed the boy to take me to the fifth floor. Vinton's room proved to be at the end of a long corridor. Even as I approached it I had no clear idea of what I was to do, yet there was no time to hesitate.

At the door I verified the number and paused for a brief instant before I raised my hand to knock. During that second the sound of voices from within reached my ears through a half-open transom.

One I instantly recognized as the voice of Vinton; the other was also that of a man, although strange to me. I withheld my knock and considered rapidly, for I had not figured upon encountering a second man. With Vinton alone, I should have knocked and forced my way into the room as he opened the door. With the odds increased, I realized the advantage to me of creating a surprise, if possible.

If Vinton had a caller, the chances were the door was not locked. I placed my hand on the knob and turned it gently. The door gave inward slightly.

I swung it open sharply, stepped across the threshold, closed it behind me, and stood with my back against it. One hand was buried in a side pocket of my coat, and grasped in it was the automatic.

The door was shut almost as quickly as Vinton could turn. He was standing before the dresser, in his shirt-sleeves, and had been in the act of adjusting his collar when the interruption came. The man's self-control was superb. I did not expect him to be frightened; but he was not even surprised, either in expression or gesture. He looked at me steadily for a few seconds, one hand still holding the loose end of his collar, then deliberately he turned back to the mirror and proceeded to button the flap into place.

"Why, good morning, Mr. Mansfield," he said pleasantly. "To be truthful as well as conventional, this is an unexpected pleasure."

"Good morning," I said shortly, holding my place at the door and watching him narrowly.

He went on in a deliberate way to tie his four-in-hand scarf, without looking in my direction, although I observed that the dresser at which he was standing was so placed that the mirror gave him a view of me.

Vinton's occupation with his toilet gave me an opportunity for a swift examination of his companion, who was seated in a chair near the window. This man was of middle age, and inclined to corpulence. His face was round and red, his heavy mustache snow-white. He stared at me in frank amazement and started to rise from his chair.

"Sit down, Purvis," said Vinton quietly. "And keep seated. Mr. Mansfield has a gun in his pocket. Haven't you, Mansfield?"

The last words were spoken as if they were casual and unimportant, merely for the purpose of having me satisfy the curiosity of the man in the chair.

"Certainly," I said.

My reception by Vinton had somewhat disconcerted me. It made me vaguely doubt who was the master.

So the stout man was Purvis! I took another look at him while Vinton perfected the adjustment of his tie.

"Take your hand off the gun," Purvis said, moving uneasily in his chair.

"Don't do it, Mansfield!" broke in the cool voice of Vinton. "Purvis is quicker than he looks. Besides, there's myself, and I'm even quicker than Purvis."

The tall man's astonishing effrontery was irritating me. I began to feel foolish.

"And now what can I do for you?" asked Vinton, after a brief pause, during which he studied with apparent satisfaction the effect of his haberdashery. "If you've come to sell your compass," he added, "perhaps we can reach terms that will be mutually satisfactory."

"Then why did you have me followed?" I demanded. "Why didn't you come to me in the first place?"

"It isn't worth while explaining," he answered placidly. "Take my word for it, Mansfield, it really isn't. And watch Purvis there! He'll steal a march on you before you know it."

A swift glance toward the stout man told me he had slipped forward to the edge of his chair, almost as if he were poised for a leap. I was getting nervous.

"Sit back in that chair, put your hands on your knees, and keep them there," I commanded sharply, drawing the automatic from my pocket and holding it where he could plainly see it.

"That's right," observed Vinton, with an approving nod, as he saw Purvis obey. "Don't let Purvis put anything over on you. And now what shall I do, Mansfield?"

He had finished with his necktie, and for the second time turned to give me his undivided attention. His tall figure seemed to tower before me until his head almost touched the ceiling. The gauntness of the man had the effect of exaggerating his height, which was at least six feet four. His long arms hung loosely and easily at his sides. He suggested sinew rather than muscle, steel springs rather than human flesh.

The expression on his face was rather pleasant than otherwise, and it annoyed me. I could feel the man's contempt for me. I think he found a little amusement in the easily read plans of Purvis, though why he had chosen to warn me of them was utterly beyond my comprehension, unless it was all part of some quickly formed design he wished to cover. He was polite, even deferential; yet I was convinced he was inwardly laughing at me.

My visit was not going at all as I had expected. I was beginning to get angry at myself, although I resolved not to make a display of temper.

"You stand right where you are, Vinton," I said, turning the automatic in his direction. "I'll do you the compliment to say I think you'll bear watching. So don't move!"

"I won't," he answered obediently.

"He doesn't dare shoot in this hotel," put in Purvis, but I noticed he was circumspect in retaining the pose I had ordered for him.

"Wrong, Purvis," said Vinton. "Mr. Mansfield would certainly shoot, if he had to. He would much rather shoot than have the two of us on top of him. In his position, I certainly should. Put yourself in his place, man. There are two to one. Why shouldn't he shoot?"

He seemed to find diversion in discussing the affair from a hypothetical standpoint.

"If you don't mind getting down to business," he added, almost apologetically, "I'd like to get through. Frankly, I want my breakfast."

"I'm not here about the compass," I answered, controlling my anger, which was only increased by the man's brazen calm.

"So? Then what are you here about?"

"Just at present, I'm representing the estate of the late Rufus Jennings," I said.

"So you were in the house last night!" he remarked quietly. "That's interesting. I knew I smelled a cigar. This man is clever, Purvis," and he turned to his companion with a nod. "He fooled me last night. Good work, Mansfield! And did you happen to be in that rear room, upstairs?"

I nodded.

"By Jove, but he fooled me, Purvis! My compliments, sir." Vinton bowed to me satirically. "I'm sorry we didn't have the pleasure of meeting there— in the dark," he added smoothly.

As I looked at the size and poise of him, I wasn't sorry; I was exceedingly glad. There was a cold, steady look in his eyes that made me uncomfortable.

"You would have needed a hard skull if we had," I said, but somehow his attitude made me feel I was only a braggart.

"Ready for me, eh? That was good. Now will you believe I have instinct, Purvis? Something turned me around and walked me out of that room. You don't believe in instinct, Purvis, but I do."

The fat man in the chair grunted unappreciatively.

"So you want the will?" he asked, turning to me again.

"Exactly, Mr. Vinton."

"Assuming that it is in this room, I suppose?"

"I'm assuming that."

"And you're correct," he replied with a nod. "It is here. Do you wish to make a search?"

"I'll let you do that, if you please."

"He doesn't trust us, Purvis," said Vinton, with mock dismay. "Well, I don't blame him. I suppose you're authorized to obtain this will, Mansfield."

The man's astonishing acquiescence was putting me more than ever upon guard. At every instant I expected some trick.

"It's in that bag, at your left, near the bed," he went

on. "If you don't want to lose sight of Purvis and me, you can easily locate it with your foot before you stoop to get it."

Without for an instant taking my eyes off Vinton, I did as he suggested, and found the bag. Keeping the automatic steadily pointed in the direction of the pair, I lifted the bag and placed it on the bed. Then my fingers began fussing with the catch.

"Push it the other way. That's it," said Vinton, as the bag opened.

I turned it upside down and poured the contents out on the bed. They seemed to be mostly papers.

"There it is, right under your hand," directed Vinton.

I groped until my fingers came in contact with a paper that seemed to be topmost on a pile.

"That's it," his voice went on.

I raised the document to a point where I could examine it without letting Vinton and Purvis out of the line of my glance. It was a will, all right. When I shook it open, I saw a red seal at the bottom of the third sheet and the curious scrawl, "Rufus Jennings."

I knew my mission had been fulfilled. It had all been so easy I was puzzled over it. I could not tell what to make of Vinton's manner, of his nonchalant surrender. In fact, the ease with which I had accomplished the job unsettled me. I felt there must be something wrong about it.

Putting the will into my pocket, I reached down and began gathering up a handful of other papers.

"Oh, now, I say!" said Vinton. "Is that quite proper, Mansfield? I don't think so. You just came for the will, you know."

I hesitated. It did seem unfair to make any further seizures. I had no scruples about the will, but this smacked a little of larceny.

"I assure you there's nothing there of value to you," he went on, "and the loss of the papers would simply involve an annoyance to me."

"I guess I've annoyed you enough," I said, dropping the handful and resuming my position against the door.

"Thank you," he replied, bowing. "And now may I ask you to bid us good morning, Mansfield? It's well after nine o'clock, I haven't breakfasted, and Purvis and I have a busy day. What time was that appointment at the War Department, Purvis?"

"Noon," answered the man in the chair.

"Noon," confirmed Vinton, with a nod. "And there are errands to run before that. To the bank, for instance; and then to see Hopper. So, you see, Mansfield, I'm really busy."

"I won't keep you from your breakfast," I assured him.

Keeping my automatic covering the two men before me, I edged over to the small table which held the telephone and which was between me and the men. With a well-placed stamp of my foot, I tore the whole instrument loose from its place on the wall above the baseboard, and it fell to the floor with a clatter.

"How unnecessary!" exclaimed Vinton in mild protest. "I had not the least idea of trying to intercept you by phoning the office, not the slightest. And now you leave me a bill for damages! Still, it was clever of him, Purvis; I grant that. And I'm afraid he's going to delay my breakfast, too."

I backed to the door and opened it. As I stepped backward across the threshold, Purvis was sitting stolidly in his chair and Vinton was bowing ceremoniously.

As I drew the door swiftly shut, I knew I had only a moment if they should pursue me. I dashed for the stairway near at hand, one I had already noted, and down this I went, two steps at a time, to the floor below, and then on to the third. Here I made my way to an elevator I knew was in another corridor.

It seemed an eternity before the car stopped at my floor, and I should not have been greatly astonished if I had seen the tall figure of Vinton shoot into sight at any instant; but I reached the lobby without molestation. Summoning my self-possession against a possible alarm, I walked slowly over to a side entrance and out into the street.

Not until I reached the sidewalk was I conscious of the fact that the automatic was still in my hand. How I had carried it so far in plain view without attracting attention I cannot imagine. I slipped it hastily into my pocket, and hailed a taxi into which I leaped.

The taxi had placed several blocks between me and

the hotel before I felt safe from pursuit. But was there to be any pursuit? Vinton's attitude mystified me beyond measure. My bold raid had been turned into a farce, with Vinton as the chief comedian. He had given up the will without a struggle; yet I could not help crediting him with some purpose in it all, something I could not understand. I was also surprised at my own lack of exultation over what I had accomplished; I was victor, but I did not derive as much satisfaction from the fact as it seemed to warrant.

I was mentally reviewing the episode of Vinton's room when the taxi drew up at the park entrance which I had given as my destination. I got out mechanically, paid my fare, and started walking along the street without thought of where I might be headed. Half an hour of this brought me into a neighborhood most familiar to me of late. As the landmarks began to impress themselves upon my eye, I suddenly realized I was within a block of Jeanette's home.

Jeanette! I wondered what Jeanette was thinking about me. What could she think about me? It was high time to find out. Explanations were due her, and the earlier the better. I turned my footsteps in the direction of her home.

As I ascended the steps, I was aware I was less equable in mind than when I had opened the door in Vinton's room in the hotel. The maid, who knew me, went upstairs to announce my arrival, while I paced to and fro in the drawing-room, nervously.

I heard a light footstep, and Jeanette stood in the doorway. Ordinarily she is a rosy girl, high-colored and in the full bloom of young health; but now her cheeks were white. She stood looking at me quietly, while I stared dumbly.

"I see the maid was in error," she said, in a cool, quiet voice.

"Error?" I repeated mechanically.

"She announced Mr. Mansfield, but I find Mr. Larned," she went on.

"Jeanette!" I cried.

"As I have never met Mr. Larned I cannot receive him." I was stupid with astonishment. "But I will ask him, nevertheless, to do me the slight favor of delivering this to Mr. Mansfield, at his convenience."

Stepping toward me, she dropped into my outstretched hand a ring. Then, with a slight bow, she turned and left the room, and I heard her ascending the stairs.

I stood like a statue. Then I managed to rouse myself, and, with a hot flush on my face, walked out into the hall and left the house.

At first I was furiously angry. My pride had been deeply humiliated. Heaven knows, after I thought the matter over in a cooler mood, I admitted Jeanette had good right to be angry; but to be dismissed in this cool, contemptuous fashion shamed me.

I walked rapidly for several blocks. As my first wave of anger began to subside, I became aware of the fact that, strangely, there was nothing of sorrow in it. All

I regretted was the sorry figure I had cut. I had lost Jeanette, but I did not feel any sense of loss.

I took the ring from the pocket into which I had dropped it, and examined it thoughtfully. How well I recalled the night I had placed it on her finger, Jeanette smiling, warm and rosy; and yet the memory aroused no emotion in me. It was like a picture of some scene I had witnessed, but of which I had not been a part.

A little girl on roller skates swung around a corner and ran into me. I saved her from an upset, righted her, and answered her jolly laugh with one of my own.

"Here's something pretty for you to play with, Fanny," I said, thrusting the ring into her hand.

Without looking back, I went on my way. What the little girl did with the ring I don't know. All I heard was her protesting call:

"My name is *not* Fanny!"

"We can't always tell what our names are," I assured myself.

And then I forgot about Jeanette, about the ring, and about the little girl whose name was not Fanny. A figure in white flashed before my mental vision. I remembered, and looked at my watch.

I hailed a passing taxi.

"Union Station, in a hurry!" I told the driver.

A traffic block when we had almost reached the station caused me to miss a Baltimore and Ohio train by the slamming of a gate when I was only a dozen yards distant from it, and I had to wait half an hour for one

on the Pennsylvania. Even when that train started,
the journey seemed interminable, although we made
schedule time to the dot.

I took another taxi in Baltimore, but as luck would
have it, a punctured tire stopped us before we had
reached the brick walls of the estate. I paid the taxi-
man, telling him not to wait, after he had put on his
spare, as I would walk the remainder of the distance.
As I came opposite the wide stretch of lawn on the
near side of the mansion, I caught a glimpse of something in a side window on the second floor, near the
rear. It was Mary.

That window, like all the others, was guarded with
heavy iron bars, against which her face was pressed
close. One hand was thrust through and was waving
frantically at me. I increased my pace to a run, and
answered her signal with a gesture. She waved her
hand more violently than ever, and I heard her voice
calling, but could not catch the words. Whatever was
the matter, there was urgent need for haste. I bounded
up the porch, and was astonished to find the door standing wide open. Entering the hall on a run, I came to
an abrupt halt at the foot of the staircase.

Seated placidly on the fifth step was Purvis, with
a blue-barreled service gun leveled nicely at my breast.

As I stood gaping at him, I heard the front door
closed and chained behind me.

CHAPTER XI

PURVIS'S small, piggish eyes were regarding me complacently. A detail that impressed me was the wonderful steadiness with which he held the gun; the muzzle never quivered. I needed no command to remain docile, nor any information to the effect that I was a prisoner.

I heard the even voice of Vinton behind me.

"Step right into the library, Mansfield," he said.

As I turned he was standing at the threshold, holding aside one of the portières and bowing deferentially, but with a mocking smile on his thin lips. I went past him into the big room, Purvis following me, with the weapon pointed at my back.

"Just a matter of precaution," said Vinton apologetically, running his hands deftly over my clothing, locating the automatic that was in a side pocket of my coat, and removing it.

He examined it with interest, remarked that it was neat and handy, and dropped it into his own pocket. I felt shame and rage within me; but it would have been folly to the point of fatality to have closed with him, as I longed to do, in a struggle for the possession of my gun. Purvis had me covered.

"Now, you can put up your gun, Purvis," remarked Vinton. "There isn't going to be any trouble. Mansfield, I am sure, will appreciate the uselessness of that."

He motioned me to a chair, and I obeyed the hint mechanically. Purvis put his big weapon into his hip pocket and also seated himself. Vinton remained standing.

"We were expecting you," he said, after an amused study of my face.

"I am able to grasp that fact," I answered, keeping my voice as even and cool as possible.

I did not propose to let Vinton outdo me in suavity. He had set an example for me, in his own room in the hotel, which I was resolved to emulate.

During a brief interval of silence I came to a swift understanding of several things. It was obvious enough, of course, that Vinton would know I intended to bring the will to Baltimore, but it now became clear he had been anxious to get to that city ahead of me. The casual talk between himself and Purvis of a day filled with engagements, and his half-humorous plea to be allowed to go to breakfast, had all been for the purpose of putting me off guard and giving me the impression I had plenty of time to return to Mary. It wasn't much of a trick, but Vinton's manner had completely fooled me.

I knew he and Purvis must have made all haste to Baltimore, figuring they could beat me in the race. Mary, of course, was a prisoner upstairs. Her frantic signals to me were an attempt to convey a warning not

to enter the house, and I had misread them utterly.
Now I was not only helpless, so far as I was concerned,
but was equally unable to help her. The trap had been
easily set, and I had walked into it like a simpleton.
Vinton probably counted on her gestures at the window
to hurry me headlong into captivity.

"It's unpleasant to submit you to the indignity of a
search, Mansfield," said Vinton. "Suppose you obviate
it by handing me everything you have in your pockets!"

To refuse meant the alternative of either Vinton or
Purvis "frisking" me, to use an old police phrase, so
I obeyed.

One of the first things I handed him was the will of
Rufus Jennings, along with some papers of my own
that happened to be in the same pocket. He received
the will with a smile, and examined it casually to see
if it were intact.

"I knew it would be here some time to-day," he observed pleasantly.

My keys, a pocket-knife, and some money he refused
to accept, indicating with a gesture of deprecation that
this was not a vulgar robbery, but he took every paper
I had.

"Why have you made Miss Donaldson a prisoner?"
I demanded, remembering the girl in the upper room.

"Don't say prisoner," he answered genially. "We
don't like that term. Miss Donaldson is in her own
house. She is, at present, in the study."

"Yes; locked in!"

Vinton shrugged his shoulders.

"That's just a detail," he said. "For the present it did not seem wise to have you and Miss Donaldson meet. Your acquaintance seems to have progressed so rapidly that a little time for reflection will probably be beneficial to both of you. Besides, within the last few hours, Miss Donaldson has developed certain symptoms of independence which it appears desirable to discourage. I feel sure they will soon disappear."

He spoke quietly, but the cold menace in his voice was unmistakable.

"May I ask how long I am to be a prisoner?" I asked. "And why?"

"Guest," he corrected. "Not prisoner. Purvis was for making you a sure enough prisoner, by tying you in a chair, but I would not hear of it. That is a vulgarity unnecessary between gentlemen. I despise the employment of force, except in cases of last resort. I am sure you will not put us to the necessity of it."

I knew I was as much of a prisoner as if I had been shackled and locked behind bars, and for the present there was nothing to do but accept the situation.

"But I will not give you a parole," I said aloud.

"Oh, I should not expect you to," he put in, smiling. "That would be asking too much. I shall simply rely on the fact that you will see the wisdom of remaining with us without protest for so long a period as we need you."

"Well, you have the will again," I answered gloomily. "What more can you get from me?"

"There is one other now who knows such a will

exists," he said contemplatively. "That may necessitate a more hurried wedding for Miss Donaldson and myself than I had proposed. And then—what else do I want from you? There's the compass," he reminded me.

"Never!" I said, shaking my head. "I wouldn't even sell to you."

"We don't have to buy now," he replied. "We shall simply take."

For some time there had been sounds of the heavy tread of some man impatiently pacing the hall. Vinton observed my listening attitude and said:

"That's only Lazare. He's an industrious chap, but impatient; thrifty, too.. He can't forget the two husky black mechanics in the garage who have been helping him, and are being paid for idleness with him away. He should get back to work without waiting for us. Now, about the compass, Mansfield. I may as well tell you right here we've heard excellent reports of it. We have great hopes of it, and I'm sure they will not be disappointed. Where is it?"

"That's a useless question," I said, dryly. "Of course I won't tell you."

Purvis's hand moved toward his hip, but Vinton checked him with a gesture.

"We're not so crude as that, Purvis," he protested. "I am sure we shall learn what we want to know without going to any such extreme."

Purvis subsided with a grunt, and Vinton turned to the papers he had taken from me, which were lying on the table. He examined a number of letters methodically, and then took up my wallet and began an inspection of its contents. In one compartment he found a folded slip of paper, and as he opened it and read it he smiled. He held it up for me to see. It was my warehouse receipt.

"I see you have a box on storage in Washington," he remarked. "It might not be difficult to guess its contents."

"But exceedingly difficult to get the box," I answered.

Vinton pursed his lips and continued his search of my wallet. One or two of the other papers interested him, and he set them aside for further examination.

"It takes a written order, of course, to obtain the box," he murmured, as if talking to himself.

"Exactly," I said, with a smile.

"Which you will not write, I suppose?"

"I certainly will not."

"I don't know that I blame you," he went on. "Still, we'll have to see what we can do. Ask Lazare to come in, Purvis."

Purvis left the room, to return a moment later, followed by a small, wiry-looking man, whose dark features proclaimed him a foreigner. He looked Spanish, but it was hard to tell, from his accent, just what was his nationality.

He had apparently been at work earlier, for his coat and vest were removed and his shirt sleeves were rolled up to the elbow. He held a wrench in one hand as though anxious to get back to work with it on the cases in the garage which I surmised had been taking his attention. He stared at me in frank curiosity and then turned inquiringly to Vinton.

"This is Mr. Mansfield, Lazare," said Vinton. "He has come to pay us a little visit."

Lazare smiled until his white, even teeth glistened, and gave me a friendly nod.

"We have just learned where his compass is," added Vinton.

The little man's eyes sparkled, and he smiled and made me a bow.

"We shall need your help for a few minutes," continued Vinton, "but I will not keep you from your work any longer than is necessary. I should explain, perhaps, Mansfield"—turning to me—"that Lazare is a man of excellent accomplishments. In some things he has qualities that approach genius. For instance, he is a wonderful penman. He may not be able to speak our language without a little of the accent that belongs to his own, but let me assure you he can write it without the shadow of an accent."

Even before he proceeded I got an inkling of what was in his mind.

"We must have a written order to obtain a certain box deposited in a warehouse," Vinton proceeded. "Mr. Mansfield does not feel inclined to write such an order, so we must do the best we can. Fortunately, he has supplied us with his signature."

Vinton took up from the table a check he had found

in my wallet. I had filled it out and signed it several days before, intending to cash it myself; but had not needed the money, and had neglected to destroy it. I was chagrined and dismayed when I saw it in Vinton's hands.

"You might start practicing the signature, Lazare, while I get the order ready. I'll be gone only a moment or two. Meantime, Mr. Purvis will act as your host, Mr. Mansfield."

Vinton left the library and went upstairs. I could hear him unlock the door of the study, where Mary was a prisoner, and close it after him. The faint sound of a typewriter explained why he had gone to the study.

Purvis, not so confident of me as Vinton, drew his big service gun the moment the latter left the room and placed it upon his knees, giving me a significant look. I could not help smiling at the man's precaution.

Meanwhile, Lazare was studying the check with a professional air. He seated himself at the library table, selected a stub pen with care, and reached for a sheet of paper. He laid the check before him, studied my signature again, and began to write. I watched him curiously, but not until he had been at work for a time did I notice he had so placed the check that the signature upon it was, to him, upside down, and that he was writing from right to left!

My amazement at this unusual performance must have attracted his attention, for presently he looked up and smiled.

"Peculiar, you think?" he asked. "It is the proper

way. Why, I know not; but it is the best way, and easier. The mind is not distracted by trying to make one letter look like another. The letters you do not notice in this way. It is just like copying a drawing. See!"

He held up the sheet of paper and I could not repress an exclamation. Half a dozen times he had written "Daniel Mansfield," the last two signatures being so startlingly like my own I could not have sworn they were not genuine, save for the fact I had actually seen them written by another hand.

"Some time you will try it," said Lazare. "It is an excellent way, truly."

Purvis was looking at the performance with as much astonishment as I, and I heard him mutter an expletive under his breath. The door of the study upstairs opened and closed, and I heard the key turn in the lock. When Vinton came into the library he held a sheet of paper in his hand.

"Miss Donaldson sends her compliments to you," he said, with the satirical look I had seen in his face before.

He went over to the table to inspect Lazare's work, and nodded his satisfaction, after comparing the check with the forgeries.

"Go ahead!" he ordered, laying the typewritten sheet before Lazare.

The little man placed the check upon it, upside down as before, and proceeded to write my name with an ease and certainty that were astonishing. When Vinton viewed the result he was clearly satisfied, for he complimented Lazare upon his work.

"Even you could not deny it," he said, holding the paper up for me to see. It was a brief typewritten order on the warehouse to deliver to the bearer the box deposited in my name, and the signature at the bottom of it was perfect. "Purvis, you'll have to take this," added Vinton, folding the paper. "Lazare can't drive the limousine, and he wants to get back to his work. I'll entertain Mr. Mansfield."

Purvis took the paper with a nod, put it into his pocket, picked up his hat and coat from a chair, and left the house. Lazare took his monkey wrench and he, too, left. I could hear him cross the porch and his feet crunch in the lawn grass, as he apparently made his way across to the garage. I was alone with Vinton.

There were times when he gave me not the slightest attention, frequently turning his back upon me as he moved about the room; yet I knew he was constantly watchful. The man seemed to possess a sixth sense. Once or twice I made a movement when his head was averted, just to test him; he always turned about immediately, not in a startled way, but quickly, nevertheless. He was feline in the ease of his movements.

More than once, when he was close to me, I could have grappled with him before he could have reached the gun in his pocket, but I had sense enough not to attempt it. In the first place, I was satisfied I was no match for the man, physically; and then, even if I had been, there was Lazare, not so far away he could not hear and respond instantly to a cry. Nothing was to be gained by an attack, unless I could strike swiftly to win, and the opportunity for that had not yet presented itself.

It was about noon when Purvis left the house, and the next few hours dragged wearily enough. Vinton never left the library. From time to time he talked commonplaces, but did not find me in a communicative mood. My thoughts were fully occupied with my own position, with what they intended to do with me, and with Mary, held a prisoner in the room upstairs.

Vinton did not speak of her again until I brought her into the conversation. The fact was forcibly impressed on my mind that I had done Mary Donaldson more harm than good by the manner in which I had played my part. I had not only failed to restore her uncle's will to her, but I had revealed to Vinton the fact that she had accepted me as an ally against him. Also the fact that I knew of the existence of the will, and the possibility of my being a witness to that fact, had made more imminent the marriage on which Vinton insisted.

"I don't want you to hold Miss Donaldson responsible for this affair," I said. "It was I who planned it. I persuaded her.'"

"I know that," he answered.

"Then why punish her?"

"She's not being punished, my dear sir. She's just being kept out of mischief for a little while."

"Until when?"

"Until such time as I see fit."

"And what are you proposing to do with me?"

"That may depend upon the result of Purvis's errand."

"Assuming he gets my compass," I said, "what then?"

"Who knows?" he answered, with a careless movement. "Nothing is settled."

"I suppose you know what you are proposing is larceny, Vinton."

He smiled at me indulgently.

"By what name would you describe your visit to me at my hotel this morning?" he inquired.

"The cases are not similar," I replied. "In that case I was acting on authority to recover—"

He stopped me with a wave of his hand.

"I'm not going to discuss the ethics of anything," he broke in. "I'm cutting out ethics for a while. They're tiresome, and, in this matter, out of place."

I subsided sullenly. Vinton found interest in the pages of a book, sitting facing me, so that I was constantly in the line of his vision. Now and then I could hear a distant hammering from the garage where Lazare and his black men were at work, opening the boxes and dragging their contents about. Once he came into the hallway, greasy and dirt-grimed, murmuring about getting some beer. Vinton asked him to bring us in something to eat. He supplied us with some crackers and beer, and appeared to be in a hurry to return to his work.

"How is it going?" Vinton asked him.

"Excellent," he answered. "I am hoping Mr. Purvis will not be delayed—or disappointed."

"I'm expecting him back between four and five," said Vinton.

It was not more than half past four when I heard a car stop out in the road, then the door opened and Purvis entered the library. With him he carried a box I recognized in an instant. Lazare's forgery had been successful. Vinton smiled as he saw the expression on my face.

"Nice work, Purvis!" he said. "Was there any difficulty?"

"Not any," answered the bearer of the box, as he placed it on the floor. "Want it opened here?"

"Better call Lazare first. This is his job, now."

The little foreigner was summoned from the garage, and when his eyes fell upon the box they kindled with satisfaction. He fell on his knees beside it, and, with a chisel he had brought, he soon had the cover removed. My aero compass was a compact instrument and not at all heavy, and as Lazare lifted it from the box he held it up and examined it with the critical eye of a man accustomed to mechanical devices.

For some time he studied it. It was maddening to sit there and watch him, but useless to protest. I said nothing. At first my fear was that Lazare, through his unfamiliarity with the instrument, would damage it, for some of its parts were exceedingly delicate. But he handled it with careful and professional fingers, now and then nodding his head as a point would become clear to him. Not once did he ask me a single question concerning it.

"Well, how about it?" asked Vinton at length.

"A most interesting instrument," said Lazare, in his precise, slightly foreign voice. "How it will work only the test will show."

"Oh, it will work!" I blurted. I had pride enough in the thing to pay this tribute.

"We can only tell by testing," said Lazare, speaking to Vinton rather than to me. "I will take it with me."

He carried it off to the garage with him.

"I want to talk with you a little," said Purvis, turning to Vinton.

"Go ahead," responded the tall man.

Purvis glanced at me significantly and back to Vinton.

"Oh, all right," said the latter, comprehending. "Mr. Mansfield won't object to stepping into the back room for a while, I imagine. He must be a little weary of my company, anyhow."

He walked toward the rear of the library, signing me to follow, and pushed back one of the heavy sliding doors that shut off the room in the rear. As I entered, he closed the door behind me and locked it. My first move was to step quickly over to the door that led into the hall. It was also locked, from the other side.

I made a swift inventory of the room. It was the only one in the house which, up to that time, I had not visited. The room ran across the width of the library and hall, and was as deep as the dining and kitchen wing I had seen. Three windows opened out on the gardens and lawn in the rear. The windows had the familiar heavy iron bars. It was evident Rufus Jennings had possessed a fear of thieves; his house was guarded as if it were a bank.

The room was given over to paintings and sculptures. I am not much of a judge of art, but it took no trained eye to perceive that Uncle Rufus had a considerable fortune invested there. The paintings were mostly landscapes, some by foreign, some by American artists. There were bronzes and marbles on pedestals, a few of them being remarkably fine copies of classic figures.

Some of the larger pictures were supplied with special electric illumination, and I turned on the switches and studied a few of them. There were signatures in that collection of fifty or sixty paintings which were a sufficient explanation of the iron bars with which Rufus Jennings had girded his mansion.

I went to the center window and looked out over the rear. It was, as I had judged in the darkness, a deep stretch. I could now see the garage, too, and the long stretch of smooth lawn behind it clear to the high brick wall in the distance. It occurred to me that that smooth lawn stretch which I had supposed held in reserve for tennis courts or something of the sort had not been put to that use as yet because of indecision as to where driveways leading to the house and elsewhere should be built. As Mary had said, the only driveway, so far, was that leading from the main road to the garage. The ground, at the side and back of the garage, clear to the wall, was as smooth as a hand and closely cropped. There was plenty of room for shrubbery and flowers, but evidently the recent owner of the place had cared little about the exterior features of his home, save for the set flower garden and some narrow flower beds I could make out along the edges of the wall, and had been content with a grass-plot.

I stood idly surveying this restricted landscaping, until I happened to glance again toward the garage,—the back of it.

As I looked, something gradually came into view beyond the edge of the building. I knew Lazare was working there, and wondered what it might be. Further and further it was pushed out, until its shape became recognizable, even though partly concealed. I recognized it in an instant, and caught my breath sharply in my surprise.

It was the upper wing of a biplane.

CHAPTER XII

THE mysterious packing-cases in the garage, the noisy labors of Lazare and the blacks, the bringing of my aëro compass to this place—all found explanation in a single swift glance.

Yet at first I could not fully take in the daring and effrontery of the undertaking. Lazare was more than an expert in mechanics; he was an aviator. It was he who was to make the actual service test of my invention. And the flying field was the back yard of the home of the late Rufus Jennings!

So far as secrecy went, the location was as good as any that could be found so near a city. The rise of ground I have mentioned effectually screened us from neighbors on one side, and the house on the other side was so far away, hidden, too, as it was, in its shelter of trees, that its inhabitants would require a glass to know details of what was going on in the Jennings place. The brick wall, too, especially along the road, was a screen from passersby. Had they searched the country over they could not have found, aside from the made-to-order runways on the professional fields, a spot more ideal for a take-off than that smooth stretch of grassy ground. Even the brick wall at the rear was far enough away so that an expert, which I judged Lazare must be, might, in a pinch, clear it with a lightly laden small plane.

I wondered about Lazare; I had never encountered his name in the literature of aviation, yet that, of course, in a country where so many hundreds of men are flying, had little significance.

Enough of the machine became visible for me to recognize it as a type familiar to me. It was not noted for speed, but for steadiness and ability to take the air under adverse conditions it had a reputation excelled by none. It was indeed known as the safest machine for the comparative novice, though I did not imagine it was for this reason Lazare had selected it.

I had used one of the same machines in experimenting with my compass; and while I could operate it with fair enough success for my own purposes, I could not claim thorough acquaintance with it—not nearly so great as I could with the less stable affair I had used during the war. Once I had thought myself a pretty good flyer; now, with planes improved as they have been since then, and older myself, I was not nearly so sure. In the quiet after-war days, I had come to realize it was always with a quiet sigh of relief I touched earth after a flight.

My flying of late had been strictly devoted to compass-testing, and I possessed neither the desire nor the aptitude for aviation as a profession. Never in my life had I flown for pleasure—certainly not in the war—and never again did I intend to fly after I had fully demonstrated that my compass would do the work required of it. I, for one, had had enough; was content to do my traveling on the ground.

As I looked over at the yellow wing, it vibrated, and I knew Lazare, concealed behind the garage, was tinkering at it. Presently he stepped out into view, to make some adjustment, and I drew back from the window so if he glanced in that direction he would not catch sight of me. The little man was whistling, contented in his task.

If the problem of making the necessary rise to clear the brick wall—his only obstacle—worried him, he did not show the least trace of that emotion. He was going about the task of assembling and getting his plane ready in a thoroughly businesslike, yet nonchalant manner.

While standing a little way back from the window, watching him, I heard the sound of Purvis's voice in the front room. He was talking rather loudly. I stepped over to the door and placed my ear against one of the heavy panels.

"There'll be nothing doing," Purvis was saying, "until the thing is tried out."

"The point is, I need some money—now," answered Vinton, speaking more quietly.

"Lazare holds the bag," Purvis went on. "His agents won't pay until he says the word."

"Isn't something due for producing the compass?" demanded Vinton.

I did not hear Purvis's reply, but it was evidently an unsatisfactory one, for Vinton went on:

"I want to see some evidence of good faith. I'm not asking for it all, but I want something. Why can't you advance me five thousand?"

"Suppose it's a failure, and nothing is paid?" demanded Purvis. "I'd be out five thousand."

"You mean to say, in that event we get nothing for our work?"

"The whole thing is a gamble, isn't it?" growled Purvis. "You've got to take your chance, along with me."

"While Lazare takes none?"

"No financial chance—no," assented Purvis grimly. "Only a swell chance of breaking his neck if that thing lams up on that brick wall down there in back."

"Which I cordially hope he'll do," remarked Vinton genially and in his pleasantest tone, "in case the compass proves to be a frost."

"If he does break his neck, we'll never know whether it's a success or not. That's another gamble."

"Why didn't he try to buy the thing in the regular way?" asked Vinton.

"He's close-mouthed about some of his reasons, but I can guess at some of them," Purvis answered. "Negotiations like that take time. The government, furthermore, has an option on this thing, and Mansfield isn't at liberty to sell anywhere just at present, although he might be later. There's an emergency

in—well, I guess you know where. If this thing
works, it might mean more than threats and rumors
as at present. It might mean real war again, with one
side far better equipped as far as its aero fleet was
concerned than any other. It's the sort of proposition,
at any rate, in which Lazare's principals can't afford
to figure in any negotiations. The fact that there was
such a compass in existence has been kept close, up
to date, and with their dilatory tactics our government
is giving somebody else a chance at something worth
while. Nobody even guesses that an attempt is being
made to get the thing out of this country. If we win,
we win big!"

"And how do we split?"

"Even."

"With me supplying all the brains and taking most
of the risks!" answered Vinton, with an unfamiliar
note of peevishness in his voice.

"That was the agreement when we began, and it
stands now," retorted Purvis with a growl. "If it
wasn't for me, you'd never have been let in on this
thing. Besides, you seem to have another prospect in
view that ought to yield something."

He said the last words with a sneer, and Vinton
caught him up sharply.

"That end of it is entirely my affair," he said, "and
is no concern of either yours or Lazare's."

"Well, in my opinion, it's got about as much dynamite in it as Lazare's little job of flying," observed
Purvis, with a short laugh.

"It doesn't worry me. Where's the dynamite?"

"In the back room."

"You mean Mansfield?" Vinton uttered a low laugh.

"That's who I mean. How are you going to take care of him? Let him in on it? If you do, it'll have to come out of your half."

"Oh, I'll take care of him!"

Vinton must have accompanied this statement with a gesture of some significance, for Purvis broke in quickly:

"Do you think you can get away with that sort of thing in this country, my friend?"

"And do you suppose I can afford to have him running around loose?" remarked Vinton easily.

"Well, I'm not in on anything like that, Vinton."

"I didn't ask you to be. That's also my affair."

The words of the tall man gave me an involuntary chill. The only interpretation I could place upon them was that I was either to be kept a prisoner indefinitely, or else quietly put out of the way. I could credit Vinton with the will to murder as easily as with anything else. Well, Vinton might murder me; but I resolved it would be only after a good fight.

And what of Mary? More than ever was she at the mercy of the tall man. The only one who had offered to help her was a prisoner. I shuddered to think of her in the hands of Vinton, to work his pleasure, to resume and complete his task of beating down her will and courage until she became a mere passive piece of flesh and blood. Of course, Vinton would let her live —for a time, at least. There was the money he could get only by marriage. After he had his grip on that— well, Heaven help her! He might have further use for her; also he might find it simpler to—

While I was standing at the door, engaged in this terrible speculation as to the fate of the captive in the room above me, Lazare entered the front room.

I gathered he was through as he was accompanied by the negroes he had had helping to lift and assemble the heavier parts of the plane.

"She's all set up," he announced. "I shall give the motor a spin. Like to see? And then, Purvis can take that roadster and drive those mechanics into Baltimore. And be sure you see them on the New York train yourself, Purvis," he added, with a snap to his tone.

Purvis grunted something and I heard the three men go out. I went back to the window where I could watch. Presently there was a series of short explosions, and that part of the plane I could see began to vibrate, as if under heavy tension. Lazare had started the engine. By the even whir it made I could tell the motor was running smoothly. After a little he shut it off.

It was not until I had heard the runabout drive off and heard Vinton and Lazare talking in the library that I roused myself from an aimless consideration of my situation, and began to look about for some manner of escape. It angered me to think I had taken my imprisonment so complacently.

The first thing I did was to hunt for some weapon. I had nothing in my pockets that would be of the least use, and I made a survey of the room to see what it might yield. A handsome bronze figure of Apollo, standing on a mahogany table, attracted my eye, and I lifted it down from its perch and hefted it. The thing weighed some thirty odd pounds, I judged, and as I grasped it by the head with both hands I found it would make a rather effective bludgeon.

I placed Apollo on the floor, near the entrance to the sliding doors, where he would be handy in case Vinton or one of the other men opened them. Then I selected another bronze of about equal weight and set it in an advantageous position near the door that led into the hall.

The only definite plan I had was this—the fight would start the minute either one of those doors was opened, no matter by whom. The first man was going to get Apollo or the Venus d'Medici on top of his skull. After that things would run according to developments. But I figured on getting one man, at least; if Vinton, so much the better.

Having made this crude provision for offense, I returned to the consideration of escape. To attempt either one of the doors while the men were in the front of the house would be folly. I turned to the windows. The bars were of inch stuff, round and securely sunk, both above and below, in stone.

I unlatched one of the windows, and raised the lower sash for a better examination of the bars. Taking out my penknife, I opened the file and tested one of them. It took but a short test to show me there was no hope there. Rufus Jennings had girded his house, not with cast iron, but with chilled steel. Even with proper tools it would have been a work of hours to make a passage through those bars.

For the sake of setting my mind at rest upon this point, I tested the bars at all three windows. They were of uniform material.

No outlet there—at least with the means at my disposal. Remained only the two doors, and these were out of the question. For a moment I contemplated attacking the wall of the house itself, but this would have been a tedious and noisy job, sure to attract the attention of Vinton or his companions. Besides, I was unprovided with implements.

It began to look as if my only chance was that of a fight and a quick dash at the first opening of a door, trusting to a surprise to aid me. Once I got clear of the house, it would be a simple matter to get aid for Mary. I did not believe Vinton would dare harm her if he knew I had escaped to bring relief.

As I paused near the sliding doors in one of my futile tours of the room, I heard Vinton saying:

"But why not to-night? There's at least an hour and a half of good light."

"I want more time than that," answered Lazare.

"It is to be a good test. And besides, my friend, I want good light for selecting a landing place. I know your country hereabouts none too well. It might not be possible to return here."

"Oh, there's plenty of level country all about here," said Vinton impatiently. "I don't like to see all this time lost, if you say everything's ready."

"Even the tanks are filled," replied Lazare in his precise tones. "There is only the compass to affix; that is the work of but a few moments. I am an airman; yes, Mr. Vinton. I take such chances as belong with the work; but I take none that are not necessary."

There was a finality in the little man's voice that must have annoyed Vinton, but I could not hear his response.

"So it is to be at daylight," I heard Lazare add. "At daylight to-morrow and no sooner."

I wondered if they proposed to leave me without molestation until then. Inasmuch as the success or failure of the test appeared to have nothing to do with my ultimate fate, there was no reason to believe Vinton would not attend to my end of the problem that very evening if he chose.

As I was surveying the back yard from the window, I saw the little figure of Lazare crossing toward the garage, carrying my compass under his arm. The sight filled me with rage, but all I could do was to stand impotently and watch him disappear behind the garage. He was there for a time, out of my view. When he emerged, he was without the compass, and I knew he must have been fastening it in place, alongside the pilot's seat. I saw him come toward the house.

A noise caused me to whirl, I ceased my unpleasant reflection and ran toward the sliding doors, thinking some one had his hand on the lock. But Vinton and Lazare were speaking softly, apparently at the farther end of the library. I listened at the hall door, but there seemed to be nobody on the other side. The noise was repeated. It sounded like a soft scraping, within the walls. It was followed by the sound of dropping particles.

I ran to the huge open fireplace, and as I dropped on my knees before it, a few bits of sooty plaster fell upon the wide hearth. I waited, breathless. There was something in the chimney!

More bits of plaster fell, and the scraping noise continued, becoming more audible each second. Now and then I could hear something knock against the bricks or stones of the flue. Nearer and nearer the sounds came, and, with a final bump, something attached to the end of a cord fell clear and dangled before my eyes.

I watched it descend until it almost touched the hearth, and reached out and took it. It was a dictaphone cylinder, used as a weight. Into it a sheet of paper had been rolled, with the cord run through to hold it in place.

Mary had sent me a message from the room above!

I gave the cord a couple of sharp jerks, as a signal to her, and felt a pull in return. With eager fingers I untied it from the cylinder and carried the message over to the window.

As I slipped the paper out I found a lead pencil had been run through it several times, like a pin, and this trivial fact conveyed a world of satisfaction to me. I did not need the pencil; there was one in my pocket. But the mere sending of one by Mary told me, as clearly as words could have done, that the girl had her wits about her, perhaps even a plan of escape, and wished to establish communication with me.

She had written:

I know they have you locked in the room below. Vinton said he was going to. I am in the study. It is useless to try the windows. But you *must* escape. I tried to warn you before you came into the house, but you did not understand. There is not even a chance at the telephone for either of us, for the only ones are in the library and pantry. If I start a commotion up here, do you think I could draw them all upstairs, while you make an attack on one of the doors? I will do it if you say. Vinton has no intention of letting you go. But *you must not* fight with him, for he is able to kill you. Never mind me, but get away yourself. Answer.

God bless her! Mary Donaldson still had her courage. Vinton had not yet broken that.

I considered her scheme, and shook my head slowly. Vinton was too clever to be fooled by it; of that I was convinced. He would probably go upstairs himself to investigate the noise in the study, but he would leave Purvis on guard below. And it would not do to precipitate a failure, for that would only be a means of insuring additional vigilance, and would probably result in the removal of Mary to a room from which she could not communicate with me. So, after pondering the matter briefly, I wrote:

It would not fool Vinton. We must try some other way. Can you send me down any sort of a weapon? Is there a pistol in the study? Whatever you send down, wrap it in a cloth, so it won't make so much noise in the chimney. I got the will, but Vinton got it back. They have my compass, and are going to make tests to-morrow morning. Aeroplane back of the garage. Keep up your courage, Mary! We'll get out of this together.

Slipping the dictaphone cylinder into my pocket, I went back to the fireplace, tied the message to the string that still dangled there, and gave it a jerk. Immediately the paper vanished up the chimney.

I sat down before the hearth and waited until a little shower of soot heralded the approach of another message. She had used a handkerchief wrapped around one of her uncle's mineral specimens for a weight. There was a folded paper inside. It read:

No weapon of any kind here. Sorry. I'm trying to think of some other scheme. You must not try to get out; that is useless. Vinton says he will make me marry him to-night. You must save yourself. Forgive me for having brought you into this. Thank you for all you have done.

Vinton was to marry her to-night! I sat glaring at the announcement in sullen rage.

"He sha'n't marry her to-night!" I muttered. "I'll call him in here and brain him first. I'll get him, if I don't get anybody else!"

But while my mind revolted at the man's devilish plans I realized I was utterly helpless to thwart them and that my muttered words were little more than a boast.

As I sat there in front of the fireplace, trying desperately to think of a method of escape, I noticed the dangling cord and its weight swinging to and fro. I idly watched the pendulumlike motion. The handkerchief, weighted with the stone, swung back and forth in an arc of perhaps two feet, without touching either side of the fireplace. In a flash, I saw the significance of it.

Lying flat on the floor, I crawled head first into the fireplace and turned my eyes upward. Far above me was a faint patch of light; not a clear vision of sky, but an indirect light, as if it entered the chimney from the sides.

I reached my hands upward as far as I could and felt the rough stones. I crawled out and wrote a message to Mary:

You won't marry Vinton to-night or any other night, unless you do it of your own free will. I'll take you out of this house with me, if I go at all. After you receive this don't send any more messages and don't be alarmed if you hear a noise. I am coming up the chimney.

CHAPTER XIII

W HEN I wrote that message to Mary I had no clear plan, nor did I have opportunity to form one later. Things just happened under the impulse of a resolve to get the girl and myself out of Vinton's grip. Just what good it would do either Mary or me for me to ascend the chimney I did not attempt to figure; only it would bring me nearer to her, and that seemed to make it worth the trying.

Although active and possessed of a healthy endurance, the acrobatics of a chimney-sweep had never been part of my accomplishments, and I did not know when I sent the message whether I could perform the feat or not. She must have been greatly astonished when she learned of my intention, but she obeyed my injunction not to send down any more messages, and was evidently waiting for me to make good my boast.

The first thing I did was to collect a couple of the heavy Oriental rugs that adorned the floor of the art-gallery, roll them up into a thick pad or cushion, and push them into the fireplace. They were to serve the double purpose of receiving noiselessly any bits of brick or stone or plaster I might break during my climb, and also of deadening my own fall, in case I should slip and come down like a plummet.

After making this preparation, I listened at the sliding doors. Purvis had made a quick trip and was back. He and Vinton were talking. Vinton was again on the subject of money, and I judged the pair had, for the time, forgotten me. At any rate, they knew I was safe behind the steel bars of Rufus Jennings's windows.

I crawled into the fireplace, turned about so that my back was against the outer wall, and stood up. In order to reach an erect position I had to lean backward slightly, as there was a bend in the flue which connected the fireplace with the main chimney. Looking up, I could see the light above me more clearly.

I felt around carefully with my hands. The interior of the chimney was, fortunately, quite rough in its finish. Had the chimney, like the house, been made of brick, and smooth, like the outer wall, there would have been little hope for me.

The main flue was rather more than two feet in breadth, its lesser diameter being about eighteen inches. This made close quarters for a good-sized man, but if it had been much larger I think I never could have climbed it. Setting my elbows against either side of the chimney, and similarly thrusting outward with my knees, I began to wriggle slowly upward.

The task of getting beyond the bend in the flue bothered me greatly. I was fearful, too, of making sounds that would reach the quick ear of Vinton, and thereby bring the whole adventure to an ignominious end. I managed to wriggle up into the main chimney, so that my feet were perhaps a yard above the floor of the art-gallery; but then I realized I should never be able to complete the ascent to Mary's room unless I adopted another method of climbing. The work was too exhausting.

Victor Hugo tells us that *Jean Valjean* could make an ascent in the angle of a wall by pressing his knees and hands against the opposite surfaces and slowly working his way up, a feat only possible because of his great strength. Well, I was no *Valjean*, and I soon found that his method was out of the question for me.

I managed, despite my cramped quarters, to get my knife out of my pocket, and began feeling around for places where I could dig plaster from between the stones, and thus make grips for my hands and toes. It was painful work and slow, and I knew not at what moment Vinton and his companions might enter the room below me; yet there was no alternative.

The business of cutting notches for my hands was simple enough, for the plaster was old and some of it fell out readily; but to find these same notches with my feet, after I had ascended a little, was infinitely more difficult; and even when I had them located it was almost impossible to get the toes of my shoes far enough into them to afford a secure hold.

Foot by foot, however, in the pitchy darkness of the chimney, I toiled my way upward. Once, when I must have been ten feet above the hearth, my foot slipped out of a niche, and I only saved myself from falling by jamming my elbows against the sides of the flue, exerting a desperate pressure while I fumbled about below me with my feet until I located one of my "steps."

I was breathing heavily, because of unusual labor, and began to choke and cough, for the chimney was filled with fine soot, likely not having been cleaned in years, and every time I made a movement the air would be filled with a cloud of it. I had one such violent paroxysm of strangling I thought I should have to give up the task, but I managed to cling motionless to precarious handholds and footholds until the soot settled and the air was fairly clear.

It was all taking time, and I felt I had none to waste. As I resumed my muscle-wearying journey another idea flashed into my mind. I had no clear notion of what I intended to do when I reached a point opposite the study in which Mary was imprisoned; but I resolved to enter that room by means of the fireplace and join forces with her against the enemy below. The thought of such respite from the choking blackness of the chimney spurred me on with fresh determination.

One of my hands reached a recess in the stonework, on the side toward the room, and I knew I was approaching the flue that led into the study. Getting both hands into it, I managed to haul myself up a couple of feet farther, so that my head was above the edge of the shelf.

About three feet below my eyes was a square of daylight, illuminating the hearth of the study. I struggled onward until I could get my knees against the recess where this second flue opened into the chimney, and, with my back braced against the outer wall, I paused, panting for breath.

She must have been close to the fireplace, listening, for I saw a shadow on the hearth.

"Mary!" I called softly.

"I never believed you could do it!" she whispered back.

Amazement was in her voice. I caught a glimpse of a blue dress, and she was kneeling on the hearth, trying to look up into the blackness that concealed me.

"Are Vinton and the others still downstairs?" I asked.

"Yes. What are you going to do?"

"I'm coming into the study," I answered, "as soon as I can get my breath."

Momentarily, I retained my cramped position, breathing heavily, and then I began the task of trying to get into the study. It involved rising to an erect position, with my feet on the edge of the flue, and then sliding down into it. I had risen and was about to take the plunge when a call from Mary halted me.

"Are you sure there is room enough?" she asked.

"There was room enough in the other flue," I answered.

"But I think this is smaller."

I bent my head downward and looked into the aper-

ture which slanted away from me, and upon the edge
of which my feet were braced. It certainly did look
smaller than the opening that led into the fireplace on
the floor below; in fact, it looked uncomfortably small.

"How wide is it?" I whispered to her. "Have you
anything to measure with?"

"Wait; I'll see."

She was gone, and then I could see her on the hearth
again. Wriggling her way into the fireplace, so that
her body cut off the light from below me, I could hear
her feeling about with her hands. Presently she slipped
back into the room and called up:

"Eleven inches at the narrowest point. I used a
tape-measure."

My heart sank. I never could make it. Against a
smooth surface and under less cramped conditions I
might possibly, by violent effort, squeeze my body
through an eleven-inch aperture; but I knew I could
never manage that flue. To slide into it, feet first,
would simply mean to jam myself fast; I should be like
a cork in a bottle, and with little prospect that I could
extricate myself. It was only her forethought that
saved me from such a disastrous and ridiculous predica-
ment.

"It's too narrow, isn't it?" I heard her ask, in a
guarded voice.

"Yes, I'm afraid so."

I tried to keep discouragement out of my voice, but
I doubt if I succeeded very well.

"There isn't any way I could help to make the opening bigger?" she asked anxiously.

"It would take hours to get those stones out—and the proper implements," I answered.

I was dismayed and almost discouraged, for it seemed that all the hardship and toil of my sixteen-foot climb had been a useless expenditure of time and energy. Mary and I were as effectually separated, so far as all the assistance I could give her was concerned, as if I had remained in the room below.

"You'll have to go back!" she whispered. "I'm afraid it's no use."

"Wait!" I said. "Let me think a bit. Could you get me a glass of water?"

She disappeared from the hearth, and was soon back, with a glass in her hand. Thrusting her head and shoulders part way into the flue, she reached upward into the chimney. I stooped, took the glass from her and drank greedily. My throat was dry and parched from breathing the soot in the chimney, and I was thirsty as a result of my exertions.

"Are there bars on the windows of your room?" I asked, as I handed back the glass.

"Yes; all the windows in the house are barred."

"The place is a dungeon!" I exclaimed despairingly.

"It seems so," her voice answered. "I'm sorry you can't get into the room. I—I'd feel a little safer, then. If you were only as small as I!"

"As small?" I echoed. "What do you mean?"

"Why, I could get through that flue," she replied

with a sigh. "I found I could when I handed you up the glass."

I felt my blood leap.

"You are sure?" I asked eagerly.

"Sure," she answered.

I turned my head upward. The light I had observed when I first looked into the chimney was nearer. I wondered if it were possible to—

Anything was worth trying, no matter how desperate.

"Mary!" I called.

"Yes?"

"Is there anything like a rope in your room?"

"I'll see."

She was gone for two or three minutes, while I stood braced in the black hollow of the chimney trying to consider calmly a daring scheme.

"There are some very strong curtain cords," I heard her voice.

"What length?"

"Perhaps thirty or forty feet, if they were knotted together."

"Knot them together," I commanded, "and then pass me one end."

She must have been busy at this task when I heard her gasp, and she called swiftly:

"Vinton is coming upstairs. Be quiet, for your life!"

I could hear the door of the study unlocked and then Vinton's voice:

"Well, have you concluded to get married without a fuss?"

Apparently she made no answer, for he went on:

"You may as well. Mansfield isn't going to help you; he can't."

I breathed as softly as I could, and prayed nothing would fall or rattle within the chimney.

"What are you going to do with him?" she asked.

"Not entirely decided," he answered in his easy, smooth tone. "It's my affair, anyhow. But he'll stay where he is until you're married, at least. Will you be ready in an hour?"

I heard her mumble a reply, the words of which I could not distinguish.

"In an hour, then," he went on. "I'll be back at that time. Do you want anything in the meanwhile?"

"Please leave me alone," she said, her voice trembling.

Vinton laughed.

"All right; I'll leave you alone for an hour. But you'd better fix up a little, if you're going to be a bride. There's some dirt on your hair and face."

The soot from the chimney! I held my breath. Would Vinton guess?

"I've been poking about among the shelves," I heard her say.

"Looking for a weapon of defense, perhaps. Was that it?"

"Yes!" she answered defiantly.

"Well, you won't find one," he said, laughing. "*Au revoir!*"

I heard the door closed and locked, and half a minute later she was back at the fireplace.

"That was a close call," I whispered to her. "Do you think Vinton suspected anything?"

"I don't think so; yet I'm never sure of him," she answered, fear in her voice. "He is uncanny at guessing, sometimes."

"Finish with the rope," I told her; "as fast as you can!"

"What are you going to do?"

"I'm going to get you out of here."

"It's impossible," she answered wearily. "But if you can save yourself, for Heaven's sake do it!"

"Listen, Mary!" I commanded. "I said I was going to get you out of here and I am. You're not going to marry Vinton, and Vinton won't find you here when he comes back. But it will take some risky work, and you'll have to keep your nerve with you. Can you do that?"

"I think so." There was doubt in her voice, however; not a doubt of her own courage, perhaps, but a misgiving as to my ability to get her free.

"You'll have to do it," I said. "We've got an hour to work in, and we ought to be able to make it."

"But how are you going to get me out?"

"Through the chimney!"

Her breath came sharply.

"You said you could get through that flue," I went on, "and I know you're going to do it."

"But I can't climb," she said hopelessly.

"You don't have to; I'll do the climbing. Have you finished with knotting those cords?"

"Almost."

I glanced up. A straight unbroken climb to the top! But I must do it.

"Find me something better than a pocket-knife to dig between stones with," I called.

"Will a screw driver do—or a chisel?"

"A chisel—and hurry!"

She reached up through the flue, handing me the implement. Also she gave me one end of the rope she had been knotting together. Her fingers were icy cold when they touched mine, and I grasped her hand and held it.

"Courage, Mary!" I whispered.

"Yes—I understand."

"Listen—I'm going the rest of the way up to the roof. When I signal you by this rope that I'm out, I want you to tie it firmly under your arms, and stand as far up in the flue as you can. Leave the rest of it to me. Do you understand?"

"Yes."

"It will be a dirty, uncomfortable trip, but you'll have to make the best of it."

"I'm not afraid," she answered quietly.

I gripped her fingers tightly, and she returned the pressure.

"Now I'm going," I said. "Wait for the signal."

"God bless you!" I heard her whisper.

I had tied the rope around my waist so it would trail after me as I climbed, and I began to gouge hand-holds with the chisel. It was an infinitely better tool than my pocket-knife. Indeed, it would need to be, for a large stretch of my painful journey was still ahead of me. With so many feet of chimney remaining before I reached the top, I felt like cursing the high ceilings of the old-fashioned mansion.

The chisel made things a little easier. My progress was no faster, but it was more sure. I could dig deeper recesses for my hands and feet. The only danger was that the noise of falling plaster might attract Vinton and his companions. I tried to drop the loosened pieces straight down, so they would not strike the sides of the chimney, trusting to the rugs I had placed below to deaden the noise of their fall. Several times I had to pause for breath, and to allow the clouds of soot to settle. I had coughing fits, and finally tied my handkerchief across my mouth and nose, as a sort of air filter. It helped, but I could not keep all of the dry, powdery stuff out of my throat. It sifted into my eyes, too, making them smart cruelly.

Little by little I continued my snail-like climb. Cutting steps with an ice-ax on the slope of some treacherous mountain, I thought, must be child's play to the task I was essaying in the blackness of that stone-walled funnel. More than once I wondered if my strength would last until I reached the top. The fear

of exhaustion put caution in me. Yet I was also becoming accustomed to working thus in the dark, and
my feet, almost mechanically, found the niches I cut
for them.

After the sixth or seventh pause for breath, I became conscious of a little more light in the chimney.
I looked upward and saw I was within a half dozen
feet of the top. I also saw something which caused
me to utter an involuntary exclamation of despair.

The chimney was capped with a slab of stone!

This, of course, was the explanation of the reflected,
rather than direct, light I had observed when I first
peered upward through it. The stone was set upon
smaller stone piers some ten inches in height, allowing
perfect freedom of draft, but effectually blocking the
chimney against the entrance or exit of anything so
large as a man's body.

I clung to my niches between the stones, staring
upward at this bar to freedom and wondering if all
my struggles had been in vain. It was sickening to
think of such a possibility.

Having gone thus far, however, there was nothing
to do but complete the remainder of the journey and
examine the prisonlike door at the end. So, setting my
teeth grimly, I resumed my work with the chisel and
slowly neared the stone cap. The light that came
through the aperture assisted me materially, and I soon
could touch the stone with my hand. I glanced out
through one of the little openings between the small

stone piers, and saw it was nearly dark, although the contrast to the utter blackness of the chimney was so great as to make the light from without seem almost blinding at first.

I ran my hand out and felt of the stone cap. It was about two inches in thickness, as nearly as I could judge; a stone I could easily have lifted if it were lying loose on the ground; but whether I could do anything with it from my present cramped position I did not know.

The first thing to do was to see whether I could loosen it. I dug away quantities of mortar at the top of each pier, continually testing the stone, with my chisel as a lever, until at last I felt it give slightly.

But I was in no position to exert my strength against it, for my footing in the chimney was too slight for that. Stooping, I began to dig deeper steps in the stonework, a little higher than those in which my feet were already placed. It was an awkward job, and I was aware of the swift passage of valuable time. But the thought of Mary in the study below me, waiting helplessly and anxiously for the signal I had promised, goaded me to work desperately.

When I had finished what I thought sufficiently secure steps, I slipped my feet into them, raised my body upward, bent my head downward, and placed my shoulders beneath the stone cap. I heaved cautiously and slowly. The stone moved. I had it clear of the chimney, and I let it settle back on the piers again.

What should I do with it? If I tilted it over on the roof some three feet below, it might cause a noise that would arouse the men. If I let it fall the other way, it might be seen by somebody looking out of a side window, although it would land on the soft turf at the side of the house and make little noise.

Inasmuch as it was rapidly growing dark, I resolved to chance the latter course. I put my shoulders to the stone again, lifted it clear of the piers, and with a quick motion of my body inclined it to one side. It hung suspended at an angle, slid off and disappeared. I heard a soft impact from the ground below.

And then I was out on the roof, drawing deep breaths of pure air and exulting in what seemed complete freedom after the narrow, gloomy prison of the chimney.

For the first time I had a chance to examine the rope Mary had constructed. The curtain cords were unusually heavy and strong, some sort of metal threading being woven in them, and easily able to bear her weight if she had made the knots secure. One of the knots was within my reach, and it looked to be adequate to the burden I intended it to bear. The others were at intervals down the chimney; I had to take them on faith.

I gave two sharp pulls at the rope. There was an answering signal. Bending my head over the chimney, I called as loudly as I dared:

"Are you ready?"

"Yes." The answer came faintly from below me.

"Climb into the flue as far as you can," I called down. "I'm going to pull you up."

"All ready!" she answered.

I climbed to the top of the chimney, braced my feet on either edge, and heaved slowly at the rope. Foot by foot it came in to me. It was the easiest part of the whole task. The burden of Mary Donaldson was light, compared to the grinding work of the last hour. Once I heard a faint call from her, and I stopped and listened.

"It's all right! Go ahead—but hurry."

There was a note of terror in her voice. Poor little girl! I could well understand her sensations, as she hung suspended by that single strand in the pitch-black funnel below me.

In short order I had her where I could reach her hands. And then Mary Donaldson was out on the roof with me, her hair, her face, her clothing grimed with the soot of the chimney, just as I was covered with it. My arms were around her, supporting her, while she clung to me hysterically, sobbing and gasping for breath.

"Score one on Mr. Vinton!" I said, patting her soot-smeared head and trying to assume a jocular tone.

"It was wonderful!" she whispered, "but, oh, so horrible!"

I could feel her shudder in my arms.

"But it's only half the job, Mary."

"Now what?" she asked, looking up at me, and then turning her eyes wonderingly to the expanse of roof.

CHAPTER XIV

"WE'VE got to get down from here some-how," I answered.

Time was becoming shorter and more precious every instant.

While I had no means of knowing just how much remained of the hour's respite Vinton had granted, I judged from the rapidly growing darkness that not much was at our disposal. And when the hour was up and Vinton entered the empty study, I knew there would be swift discovery of the route we had taken, and equally swift pursuit.

Mary released herself from my arms, but clung tightly to my hand as I made a survey of the roof. It was almost flat, of the old-fashioned, wide-shingled variety, the mossy, green surfaces of which afforded easy footholds, and was unbroken save by a small trap door near the eaves in the rear, that opened into the slightly raised scuttle. From its roof, the house seemed more isolated than it had before. It flashed over me how easy an escape might be across the house-tops in a solid block of dwellings; but this one stood alone, far in the country. There was no such refuge.

I examined the wooden door of the scuttle and found it could be lifted from the outside.

"Shall we try going down through the house?" I asked.

"No! No!" she whispered fearfully. "We could never do it!"

"If I only had a weapon!" I said, contemplating the puny chisel in my hand.

With a gun I would have chanced an escape by way of the scuttle, trusting to a surprise to get us clear; but with no arm of any kind I knew Mary was right, and that the attempt would be folly.

I went across the roof to the front of the house and looked over. Nothing but a sheer drop there, for the columns of the Southern Colonial porch rose past the second floor and ended under the edge of the roof. Strangely enough, but three windows had been let through the wall on one side of the dwelling, and four on the dining wing side. The rear was similar to the front, being broken at regular intervals with strongly barred gratings, but of course, without the porch. It was the only side of the house, too, where the windows on the ground floor were directly under those of the second story.

I looked at Mary, who stood close at my side, and then at the rope, which bound us together like a pair of Alpine climbers.

"Thank God for the barred windows!" I exclaimed. Her puzzled expression showed she did not understand.

"You'll see!" I added, in a burst of excitement, as I began to unfasten the rope from my waist.

"I don't understand," she said.

"We can escape by them," I cried, working feverishly at the knots in the rope. "Don't you see? I can let you down to one of the study windows, and you can cling to the bars, standing on the sill, until I can get down. We can repeat the job to the art-gallery windows, and be within a few feet of the ground."

"You think we can do it?" she asked doubtfully.

"Easier than the chimney. Those will be the safest windows, too, for there will be no one in the rooms."

"Yes," she assented decisively. "Some one would be sure to see us from any of the other windows in the house."

"Let's go, then."

I looked down over the eaves at the rear. There were three windows on each floor, with the mate of each directly below it. Descent by one set of windows was as feasible as by any other, the only thing to dictate a choice being some object on the roof to which I could attach my rope.

I glanced at the scuttle, noted it was over the center windows, though the line straight downward would land one in the deep areaway, and it was that scuttle that compelled selection of the center windows. Certainly the scuttle was firm, and appeared the right thing for our purpose.

"Here's where we go down," I said, "and it must be quick work. You're not afraid?"

"Not if you tell me it's all right," she answered.

"It is," I said emphatically.

The rope was still tied under her arms, and she stood quietly, awaiting my orders. There was something brave, yet resigned, in the girl's slender figure. She had placed herself absolutely in my hands, with full trust.

"I shall let you over the edge until your feet reach the sill of the study window," I explained. "Then you must hold tight to the bars until I get down. Can you do that?"

She nodded.

"Just have confidence in me," I added, as I made sure the rope was securely fastened to her.

"I have," she said simply.

I retied the rope around my own waist, passed it around the scuttle and, nearing the eaves, I laid prone at the edge of the roof, with Mary suspended in my arms.

"All ready?"

"Ready," she answered.

There was a pale spot on one of her cheeks, which the grime of the chimney had missed. An impulse seized me, and I bent my head close to hers and kissed the spot. She looked at me with her great dark eyes, smiled faintly, and murmured:

"Lower me! I'm not afraid."

I swung her clear of the eaves and began paying out

the rope slowly. It was but a few seconds' work, that stage of her descent. I saw her grasp the bars at the study window and swing her feet in toward the sill. She called in a low tone:

"All right!"

To reach the sill myself was a different problem. We did not possess rope enough for me to make one end fast around the scuttle, and our descent, therefore, had to be accomplished by stages. Furthermore, while it had been demonstrated that the makeshift affair of curtain cords would sustain Mary, I was not at all sure it was strong enough to carry me.

I untied the rope from my waist and threw the loose end downward. This gave me a double thickness as far as the study window below. After testing it with my hands and concluding it was strong enough to bear me, I grasped the double thickness of rope, swung myself over the edge, and went down, hand over hand, until I found myself on the window-sill with Mary, clinging to the bars.

She smiled and nodded at me bravely as I reached her side. I rested there a moment, passing my arm outside of her to make her more secure, and then began hauling in on that section of rope which was attached to her, having loosened the end fastened to me. This free end ascended, passed around the scuttle, and I caught it as it fell.

"Now for the next window," I said. "It's simply the same thing repeated. Pity those windows of the art-gallery are so far from the ground, and right above the areaway. We can't take a chance on going all the way—I'm afraid of the length of our rope. We'll have to make a stop-over at the art-gallery, too."

It was not so easy for me to lower her, however, because of my restricted position on the window-sill. One arm I had to devote to the job of clinging to the bars. I solved the difficulty by passing the rope around one of the bars a couple of times, which furnished enough resistance to enable me to manage it with one hand.

Mary swung clear from the sill and resumed her descent as I carefully paid out the rope. I was beginning to gloat over the comparative ease of this method of escape, when I heard a startled exclamation from her. She was swinging opposite the window, less than a foot from the sill, and I saw her figure bathed with a yellow light which came from within the art-gallery.

"It's Vinton!" she called to me, in a frightened whisper. "He's discovered your escape."

Here was a situation calculated to cause dismay in the heart of any hopeful fugitive. I was perched on the sill of a high second-story window, with a girl swinging below me at the end of a rope, and our enemy was already on the scent.

"Does he see you?" I called

"Not yet, I think," she exclaimed, grasping at one of the bars of the window and trying to swing herself to one side, so that she would be out of his view in case he happened to glance toward the window.

"Steady, then," I commanded. "I'm going to lower you all the way into the areaway."

I let the rope run rapidly for a few feet, carrying her past the lighted window, and checked her descent until her feet touched the concrete areaway leading out from the cellar, immediately beneath the art-gallery windows. I breathed a sigh of relief when I realized the rope had done its work—had been long enough to get her that far. I had little of the rope left in my hand, though.

"Untie yourself, quick!" I called sibilantly.

It was getting so dark I could scarcely see her figure below me, but I quickly felt the rope dangle loosely and hauled in on it. I made the same double thickness for myself as on the first stage of the journey, by passing the rope around one of the steel bars, and started to go down.

The light was burning brightly in the art-gallery as I reached the window, and I wondered if I could get past without Vinton seeing me. It would be necessary for me to pause on the sill and cling there while I freed the rope above me and repeated the operation. As my feet reached the stone support, I looked into the art-gallery through the heavy grating.

Vinton was rising from his knees in front of the fireplace, an expression of rage and cunning on his face that made me shudder. Purvis was standing gaping near the doorway, and as I paused on the sill Lazare came running into the room, evidently called there by the alarm.

"They'll examine the study above next," I muttered to myself. "That will give us a little more time!"

But not even that respite was to be granted us. As I worked madly at the rope, Lazare's quick eye, which was surveying the situation in the room with lightning speed, glanced toward the window and caught sight of my figure, illuminated by the light from within. I saw him point at me and say something.

Vinton's eyes followed the direction of Lazare's gesture, and he saw me. Without hesitation, and with a motion so quick I could hardly follow his hand, he whipped out an automatic and fired at me. The bullet passed through the glass and sung by my ear at a distance of not more than three inches.

Before I could make a move, a second shot followed it. I think it was closer than the first, but the only damage it did was to dash a few bits of glass in my face. To cling to my window perch while I adjusted the rope was to invite a sure hit from my own automatic, for that was the weapon in Vinton's hand.

"Look out below!" I shouted.

I loosened my hold on the steel bars, swung my feet clear of the sill, and dropped. A third bullet passed harmlessly over my head.

I landed feet first in the concrete areaway, sank to my knees with the concussion, a sharp pain in one ankle proving I had not escaped entirely without some injury. Mary stepped swiftly aside as I dropped, but she rushed forward and upheld me to prevent an ugly topple onto the concrete.

"Hurry!" I cried, struggling up.

I seized her hand and, limping, in spite of set teeth and my determination, hurried up out of the areaway onto the lawn.

"Make for the garage!" I shouted. "The limousine! It's in the driveway outside."

Making what haste I could, together we raced toward the garage. Mary was fleeter of foot than I, for there were sharp pains in my ankle, and I was jarred as a result of my fall into the areaway.

"Go ahead!" I commanded. "Get her started! I'll make it!"

I tripped over a coil of clothes-line that had been left on the grass outside the kitchen wing and went sprawling, so she was at the car ahead of me, and had leaped into the driver's seat when I arrived. I saw her look of despair as her hands fell limply into her lap from the instrument board.

"What—" I started.

"The key!" she panted. "Vinton's got it!"

"It'll have to be the runabout, then! Where's the garage key?"

Mary was out of the car and in one swift movement had retrieved the key and thrown open the garage door.

As I glanced over my shoulder at the house, the light was still burning in the art-gallery, but there was nobody at the windows. I knew Vinton and his companions were on their way. It could only be a matter of seconds.

I could hear Mary, in the darkness, madly trying to

get the runabout started. I heard her quick breath-
intake of despair.

"Hurry!" I urged. "There's not a second!"

But before I had finished my tumbling words, she
was out of the car and at my side.

"It—it won't start!" she choked. "No gas, probably. Oh, what—"

I seized her and pulled her outside the garage.

"Then you'll have to make a run for it! Make for
the nearest house. Vinton won't know you're not with
me, and you'll get start enough to make it hard for them
to find you in the darkness, if they follow—"

She whirled on me.

"And you?" she asked sharply.

"Oh, I'll get away all right. They won't do much
when they know there's possibility of help arriving
soon. Don't be crazy, Mary. Once you're away, you
can get help for me. Never mind me, anyway! You
do as I say!"

"If you can't go, I won't!"

She said it quietly enough, but her tone was stubborn and final. There was no time for reply. Shadowy
figures were dashing across the grass; hoarse voices
shouted imprecations. We could not be seen in the
dark, but quick chance shots zoomed by us and over our
heads.

One second to go!

And there went glimmering my vague hope I could
somehow hold the men off single-handed until the fleet-
footed girl could get away.

With a quick movement I would not, had I had time to think, have believed possible in one lamed as I was, I recovered her wrist and pulled her inside the garage. It was our last stand. In less time than it takes to relate, I had dropped into place the heavy bars that secured the doors from the inside.

With one accord we drew deep breaths of respite and fell back instinctively as there came the sharp impact of heavy bodies against the barred door. That it was but a respite, we only too well knew, for Vinton was not the man to let a mere garage stand in his way, if he had to burn the place.

I heard Mary fumbling along the wall.

"Don't!" I cried defensively. "No light, for God's sake!"

"Right!" she agreed succinctly. "Light is what we do not need."

The cursing outside died down, and I could hear a muffled mumble of conversation. A consultation, in all likelihood. I wondered, in a strangely detached way, what their next move would be. It didn't seem greatly to matter, for now there was nothing further I, unarmed as I was, could do. The thoughts whirled through my brain as I groped my way along the walls and my hand came in contact with what was probably a tool chest—locked! Not even a jack could I discover. Lazare had either left all his tools outside where he had been at work, or else he was a tidy, as well as an industrious body, and had carefully locked them all away. I could find nothing but a few bits of board which would have been as useless as my bare hands to cope with three armed men.

I heard Vinton's voice call out in ironic command:

"You may as well come out, you two! It won't go so easily with you if I have to come to take you!"

I had no time to answer. Mary spoke first.

"Take us!" she retorted, defiantly, and there was no hint of tremor in her tone.

Vinton wasted no more words. He would not. I heard his voice in a command to one of the other men, but could not make out what was said. I was not to be long in finding out.

Crash! Bang!

The heavy garage doors shivered and moaned in complaint at the impact against their timbers of something used as a battering ram with all the force of three desperate, husky men behind it. I could guess one of the heavy iron house-door bars had been requisitioned.

Crash! Splinter!

Three more Titan blows and the bar crashed through a panel.

I could hear Vinton cursing the darkness that made it impossible for him to see us.

"Well, at least they won't get a light!" whispered Mary. "I've got the button." She reached for my hand and I felt the electric light button she had untwisted in that moment she had fumbled beside the fixture.

"They can get us in the dark," I said morosely, as

I heard the panels splintering. I felt like a rat in a trap.

It was maddening to be so helpless. I stumbled through the dark to another side of the wall in a final futile search for a weapon.

I heard Mary at the rear door of the garage, fumbling with its spring lock. I hobbled my way over to her.

"The plane!" she called excitedly, her lips close to my ear.

A fraction of time I hesitated, dazed by the idea.

"Are you game for it?" I cried.

"For anything!"

"It may mean death."

"Better that than—"

I waited for no more, but grabbed her hand as the door swung open and snapped shut behind us, and hobbled along hurriedly toward the plane, trusting to opportunity and a lucky chance to get the machine moving. That the men would not be far behind us I knew well, for already the front door of the garage was crashing in, the noise hiding the rear door's opening and closing. For, in their excitement, the men had forgotten there was more than one entrance to the garage. I felt sure the only thing that had so far saved us from a fusillade was the darkness, and it must further befriend us.

We had not quite reached the plane when I heard shouts inside the garage; caught glints of what was evidently the pocket flash with which our escape had been discovered, and heard Vinton's vicious roar: "Fools! They've got out the back way! After them!"

I heard the rear door flung open; saw the three men catapult themselves into the darkness outside. There was barely time for me to flatten Mary and myself in the space between the plane and the garage wall, with our faces against it, before they dashed out into the open, Vinton's flashlight flickering here and there. I can only lay it to a lucky chance our presence was not discovered, but from the tall man's words I could gather why he did not look so near our recent stronghold.

"Think they've got away, do they?" he snarled. "Well, they won't go far!"

"Quiet, for your life!" I whispered to Mary, though I doubt if I could have been heard had I spoken aloud, the curses of the duped men were so vigorous. Vinton was barking orders:

"No use going to the house. They've had enough of that. And they couldn't get out the gate in the rear wall. They've gone by the road. You, Lazare, beat it up the road toward that house in the trees. Purvis, you cut across the road through the field. I'll go toward Baltimore myself. It's the most likely way, and I've got the limousine. And don't be afraid to use those guns!"

In spite of the desperation of the situation, I could barely suppress a grin of exultation at those orders, for in a few moments I would be free to use that lucky

chance for which I had hoped. With a deep breath
of satisfaction I heard the purr of the motor as Vinton
shot out into the road and could guess he had already
seen the other men on their way. Three, four more
silent minutes I waited, and knew the time for action
had come. If I could start that plane at all, I could
do it in five minutes.

Whether everything was clear or not, I did not know,
and there was no time to investigate.

I thrust Mary up beside the pilot's seat, leaped in
beside her, and groped for the self-starter I knew would
be within reach if the machine was rigged like its mate
I had been using. I found it. An answering roar
told me the propeller was revolving, and the machine
quivered like a live thing. I reached for Mary's hand
and pressed it firmly about the stick.

"Hold her as true as you can," I explained hastily,
"when I kick out the first block. I'm going to make
a jump for it when I kick out the other."

How hazardous this was I had no time to think,
nor whether it was possible. However, there being
nothing else to do, it was Hobson's choice, but I don't
believe any dare-devil movie stunter ever made a more
desperate leap for life than I did toward that cockpit
when, with a bound, the plane shot forward. I caught
with one hand, thought my arm was being torn from
its socket, and completely forgot my lamed foot that
jerked along the ground. I held on grimly and pulled
myself over the edge and wriggled into the pilot's

seat. In the same movement I had the stick, which Mary had held, gripped in my own hand.

"Hold tight!" I shouted, as we shot forward.

Even above the roar of the motor, I could hear hoarse, angry shouts, nearer and nearer. Too late they had thought of the one thing that had escaped them. Too well had Lazare's work of preparation been accomplished, as far as the plane was concerned.

There came a volley of shots, but Vinton and his companions had vanished from my mind. I was facing the problem I doubted even Lazare's ability to accomplish—that of clearing the rear wall with a quick ascent. For a millionaire's fortune I could not have been hired to attempt it in cold blood, even in daylight. And now I had a passenger!

The plane gathered headway swiftly. I could see only blackness ahead of me, and I did not dare take an inch more of run than was needed.

Clenching my jaws grimly, I gave a sharp jerk at the stick, and the plane tipped upward at an angle that threw me violently backward. We were in the air!

Something ominous and black slipped beneath our feet. We had crossed the high brick wall.

CHAPTER XV

F OR perhaps a minute I allowed the machine to rise steadily at a dangerously sharp angle; then I slowly adjusted the controls until we were on a horizontal course.

I ventured a look at Mary. She was huddled into her seat beside me, her silhouette outlined darkly against the sky, one hand clinging to the edge of the cockpit. Her dark curls were blown straight back by the gale which was of our own making; her short skirt was flapping wildly.

"Reach that belt on the cockpit floor if you can," I shouted, inclining my head toward her and trying to make my voice rise above the noise of the roaring propeller.

She heard me, for she leaned forward cautiously, tucking the flying skirt underneath her, and reached for the leather pieces on the floor. Lazare indeed had everything in readiness. I even sighted, beside the belt, a tightly corked bottle which I took to be the red wine which is the Latin's necessity.

When Mary sat back she held the belt. As deftly as though she were accustomed to its use, she docilely obeyed my signals to fasten it in place about her waist.

236

I felt safer for her when she had accomplished that, and more free to give all my attention to the plane. It needed it all.

As airplanes go, it was a slow-moving, but fairly safe craft; yet we were making at least seventy miles an hour, I judged. Cautiously, in the darkness, because I had not as yet located the light for the instrument board, and investigation showed me I owned not even a match to help, I ran my hands over the mechanism within reach of the pilot's seat. Everything appeared to be rigged in standard fashion. It was a brief consolation to know we were not aloft in a plane altogether unfamiliar.

Above, the stars were bright and clear, and the slender crescent of a young moon was still visible near the horizon. Below, the lights of scattered houses, and the distant luminosity of Baltimore flashed. I put two or three hundred feet more between us and the earth. The engine was running true and even.

My head was beginning to grow cooler and I had an opportunity to think more of our extraordinary situation. As I have said before I do not set myself up as much of an aviator in these days, in spite of my war experience, save that I had, more recently, without breaking any bones, made a number of flights for the purpose of testing an invention. Not even in the war had I been called on, as a pilot, to make a night flight. Yet here I was, suspended above an unknown territory, with only the stars and a faint show of moonlight to guide me—and a girl with me!

I had to give Lazare credit, for the machine was acting well. I tried no experiments with it, though; it was no time to be venturesome. As we ran on steadily, without pitching or tipping, my confidence waxed.

At first I took no note of our course, but held on steadily cross country. The infrequency of the lights told me we were getting still further from the city than was the Jennings' mansion. I glanced at Mary. She had leaned forward a little, so that her chin extended over the edge of the cockpit, and her eyes were staring directly downward. I was afraid she would become dizzy, and shouted to her to close her eyes.

She shook her head, turned her face toward me, and—there was still enough moonlight for me to be sure of it—smiled. Her lips framed something, and I leaned over as far as I could to catch the words. All I could hear was:

"And wonderful!"

There was a woman for you! Vinton, the gloomy house, the terror of the chimney, all the mad dashing about like a trapped animal, had vanished from her mind. She was exulting in a new and glorious experience!

I was thankful she realized nothing of our real danger, but had a mind only for the excitement of the adventure and the thrill of an exhilarating sensation. For myself, I could not dismiss our peril from my mind. Even an expert airman in my place would not have relished the situation. I feared that the tanks, even if there were gas enough in both, might not hold enough to carry us on until daylight, and if the engine ran true. I could tell nothing of the gas, for I knew no more of the location of the gauge on the instrument board than I did of that of the dash light, and had no time for exploration. On the other hand, the hazards of an attempted landing in the darkness were too great to be considered with equanimity.

Furthermore, I knew little or nothing about the country below us. All I could make out from our present elevation—and I did not care to make a closer inspection—were occasional farm houses and barns, groves of trees, rolling bits of clearing, and now and then a low hill. I had seen no unobstructed field of sufficient size or flatness to tempt me to alight; indeed, if we had passed over any I might easily have missed them in the gloom.

It was not until we had been going for at least a quarter of an hour, leaving the more settled country farther and farther behind us, that I thought of my compass, and I laughed aloud in joy. A test to the last point—a real test! The compass would guide us.

There was a small storage battery attached to the compass, with a bulb for illuminating the dials, though I had never before needed artificial light. I felt for the switch and turned it. A glow of white light fell on the instrument, and I bent over it.

I could not suppress a cry of dismay. Two of the dials were shattered, and the remaining one, which indicated only the side drift of the machine, was utterly useless and meaningless without the others. Lazare had bungled the job of installation, and had wrecked it! I bent closer and saw what had really occurred.

A bullet, either from Vinton's automatic or from Purvis's big service pistol, fired wildly at us in the dark, had hit the enclosing case and hopelessly destroyed the recording dials. The compass, for all the use it was to me, might as well have been safely in storage in Washington. I was aloft in the night with nothing to steer by but the stars.

No longer was even the slender crescent of the moon visible. A chill of fear came over me. What if we were going eastward? It would not take many miles of travel in that direction to bring us out over the sea. And once over the sea—well, that would be the end!

I adjusted the controls and ascended, trying to locate the pointers of the Big Dipper, from which I might get a line on the pole-star. But I knew practically nothing of astronomy, and the diamond-like dots in the black sky were so multitudinous and confusing that none seemed familiar to me.

Climbing, I let my glance sweep the horizon, and over my shoulder, at last, I caught a glimpse of the moon that had evaded me. I had been gradually describing an arc without knowing it. I carefully swung the machine about until we were headed directly toward the silver crescent. That was at least in a general westwardly direction and away from the sea.

I knew the moon would last but a little while longer, and I did not care to fly higher, to keep it for an additional time for a guide. So I marked above it, at a considerable height in the sky, a bright star, directly to the left of which were two others of somewhat lesser brilliance. This group I fixed in my mind as marking the west, and I made up my mind to keep the machine, at any cost, pointed steadily in that direction.

I began to be concerned about our elevation, and recalled the barograph attached to the compass-box. I twisted the little flexible arm that held the electric bulb around to illuminate the instrument, and was relieved to see it had escaped damage. It recorded an elevation of eleven hundred feet, for we had been climbing slowly but steadily in my hunt for a guiding mark in the sky.

We were at a greater height than I desired, or than was necessary, and it was no longer easy to discern anything on the dark surface of the earth. I let the machine dip at a gentle incline until the barograph registered four hundred feet, and resumed a horizontal course, keeping a close eye on the instrument.

Presently we passed over a town of considerable size, but I could not determine from our general course just what place it was. A few minutes later we went midway between two villages, probably about two miles apart, and then we were in the open country again, which fast became more desolate in character, until I discerned nothing but dark woods.

Keeping the starry triangle as my guide, I let the machine drive onward into the night, eagerly searching the dim earth beneath us for a safe haven. A soft touch on my shoulder caused me to turn with a start that made the plane rock slightly, although with the automatic ease of a bird it immediately returned to an even keel. Mary had leaned toward me, and had her lips close to my ear.

"Where are we going?" she shouted.

"Westward," I answered, my eyes fixed on the goal in the sky.

"By your compass?"

I shook my head; it was useless to tell her we were as good as lost in the air. But she persisted.

"Doesn't it work?"

"Hit by a bullet," I shouted at her. "Sit still!"

"How far shall we fly?"

That was a question beyond my ability to answer. It depended upon the quantity of gasoline Lazare had put into the tanks, upon the reliability of the motor, upon our freedom from the hundred or more mishaps that may befall the aviator. Of one thing I was sure. I had no intention of remaining aloft a minute longer than was necessary to discover favorable ground beneath us.

It might be just as well at that to discover whether there was any gas at all in the second tank. There was the possibility it had not been filled, since Lazare had been planning only for a short test flight, and it flashed over me that the reason there had been no gas in the runabout was that the foreigner had drawn it off for the plane. What if there had not been enough for two tanks? And we were using what there was in one tank at a great rate.

I turned the button that switched off the tank we were using, and switched on the other. A spitting of the engine answered, and I quickly switched back.

"See if you can reach the tanks and find out if the caps are on both," I shouted at Mary.

She reached her arm over the back of her seat to the tanks behind us and in a moment withdrew it. She raised her fingers to her face, then put the hand close to my nose.

"The cap's on tight, too!" she screamed into my ear. Gasoline!

The discovery startled me so that had the plane been a tricky one, I believe I should have upset it then and there. One of the tanks was leaking; perhaps both! Our fuel was disappearing; I could not tell how rapidly.

"Tank leaking!" I howled at her. "See if you can find it."

I did not dare try to locate the leak myself, but instead, as her hand groped again toward the tanks, I bent my eyes earthward. We were still passing over what seemed to be an unbroken forest, although the darkness doubtless aided in the illusion.

I saw her turn from the tanks and bend over, fumbling about her feet. I could not waste my energy howling at her in that position, but wondered why she should be interested in her shoes at such a time; or if it were possible the gasoline were leaking into the cockpit. It hardly could, I reasoned. She did not attempt to speak to me as she rose and got partially to her knees to bend over the tanks that held our precious power-supply. She sank back into her seat, leaned toward me and cried, her voice raised shrill above the noise of the propeller:

"I found it! Stopped it with my handkerchief wrapped around the stopper of Lazare's red ink."

"Only one tank?" I shouted.

"Only one," she answered. "It was a little round hole."

I understood. The plane had been struck by more than one bullet. Not only was my compass wrecked, but the marksmanship of Vinton or Purvis had robbed us of fuel, too; how much, only time could tell. What a marvel it was that neither of us had been hit! And that no vital part of the plane had been damaged!

More vigilantly than ever I kept watch below for clear spaces. The reduction of our cruising radius might prove the greatest sort of a calamity, if the character of the country over which we were passing should continue unfavorable. I did not care to alarm the girl by telling her my fears, although I have not the least doubt she divined the situation without any explanation from me. She resumed her position with her chin over the edge of the cockpit, her eyes turned downward.

Presently I heard her cry out. She was pointing below us. I craned my head forward and followed the direction of her finger. The outlines of the earth had disappeared. All I could see was something that seemed to match the sky above, save that there were no stars in it.

It was impossible for us to have risen far without my knowledge; at any rate, so far as to lose the outlines of things below us. I turned and consulted the barograph. It registered only four hundred and fifty feet.

All around beneath us, the same smooth, opaque surface. Could it be water? I could think of no such extensive sheet so near Baltimore, to the west; whatever this was, it spread out below us as far as the eye could reach in the darkness.

Puzzled, I allowed the machine to dip gradually, keeping my eye alternately on the barograph, which recorded our varying altitudes, and upon the curious phenomena below. Four hundred, three hundred and fifty, three hundred feet. No sign of earth.

I slid down to the two-hundred-and-fifty-foot level, but could not see a single landmark. I glanced upward to find my guiding stars, and failed to find them. More than that, every star had vanished from the sky!

I became conscious of a damp coolness on my cheek and the sensation of chill through my thin coat. I understood. We were in a fog!

The barograph was reading only two hundred feet. It was time to ascend rapidly. At three hundred feet I could discern faint white dots about us; at three hundred and fifty we were out in the clear sky, and my triangle of stars was visible ahead of me. I kept on to the four-hundred-foot level, and then let the machine drive ahead on an even keel. Below us the earth was invisible, completely covered by a thick layer of night fog.

Fine business! Night, a fog, unknown country beneath, a doubtful gasoline supply—and no compass!

Involuntarily I glanced at Mary. She chanced to glance up at the same instant, and gave me a swift nod, as if she comprehended the situation; yet there did not seem to be the least trace of fear in her. Should I tell her the true state of affairs? I doubted if there was need to. She seemed to understand. I knew she did when she bent nearer and called:

"Anything is better than Vinton!"

Thank God, she was brave about it! Although I had little time for anything save the operation of the machine, I none the less felt that at last I was obtaining a true glimpse of the woman's real spirit. It remained unbroken, despite the sinister, relentless attacks upon it by the tall man who was our evil genius.

Westward we flew at four hundred feet, the same even, unbroken layer of fog beneath us. The whole earth was plastered with it! We might have passed villages, even cities, but they were invisible. The air was perfectly clear at our elevation; there was not the slightest dimming of stars; but below, the screen of mist was as impenetrable to the eye as the steel armor of a battleship. I dared not attempt a landing in it; what sort of earth surface it concealed was beyond a guess.

Yet at any time I might have to land, from sheer

exhaustion of power to keep us aloft. Four hundred feet beneath us was solid earth, yet we might not touch it. Fog was a contingency against which even my compass would not have availed, so far as the selection of a landing spot was involved. We had escaped Vinton —for what?

For half an hour we flew above the crest of the fog. Sometimes it thinned out, so that it seemed far below us, even at our moderate elevation; at other times it piled up in ridges, into the tops of which we plunged, forcing me to rise in order to regain a vision of my starry guides. Once we were carried to six hundred feet to escape it; at another time I let the plane slide down to the two-hundred-foot level and was still above the bank of mist.

Not a light shone up from below. Once, when we were at a low level, both of us distinctly heard the clanging of a bell. It sounded like the gong of a motorman, but it faded away, and we heard only the incessant roaring of the propeller that drove us on. The mockery of it was the brilliantly clear sky overhead.

We had been voyaging above the fog for an hour, and I estimated we had been in the air for at least half as long again. Baltimore must be seventy or eighty miles or more to the east of us, allowing for all the circling we had done, and I began to wonder vaguely just where we were. For the life of me I could recall nothing of my geography.

The air was cooler, and the rapid pace at which we were passing through it had chilled me. I felt pity for Mary, who was without even a coat, and would gladly have given her my own, had I dared try to accomplish its removal. She gave no signs of suffering, however, but sat motionless, her hand tightly gripping the rim of the cockpit, and her eyes bent steadily downward.

My ear caught an ominous sound. The engine missed. I listened intently. It skipped three in rapid succession. I knew what that meant. We were running on dregs of gas. Our flight would soon be over. Where and how would it end?

Mary's quick ear noted the uneven explosions, and she leaned closer, facing me, until I could see the look of inquiry in her eyes. The explosions were more and more intermittent.

"We must land!" I called to her.

She nodded understandingly.

"Don't be afraid," I added, yet my heart was in my mouth as I advised her, for I believed death lay beneath us.

She smiled at me!

Bending over I saw that the barograph registered three hundred feet and a trifle more. The motor was spluttering and coughing asthmatically, we had begun to slow down and were losing headway. It was a matter of seconds, not of minutes. If we were not to fall like a stone, it was imperative to glide earthward— into the fog.

I set my jaw grimly and tightened my hold on the stick, just as the engine gave a final snort and stopped dead. It was volplane or fall. The end, in either case, would probably be the same; but I took the last desperate chance left, and tipped the machine downward at as gentle an angle as I dared, so we should not lose steerageway or the sustaining rush of the air.

We sped downward through the fog. The cool, wet texture of it was like a shroud of death. The particles of moisture beat against my face like fine rain.

"Hold tight!" I shrieked.

Mary obeyed me without a word.

I bent my head forward to catch the first sight of earth. Long, black tentacles stretched up toward us through the gray mist, like the arms of a gigantic squid. The plane brushed like a whirlwind through the upper branches of a tree. It staggered sickeningly, leaped clear of the limbs, and shot out into the fog.

The mist gave way to blackness. I tugged sharply at the stick as we hit the earth with an impact that exploded one of the rubber tires on the wheels beneath the plane like a pistol shot. We plunged forward with a bound that must have carried us fifty feet before we touched again.

We started another mad leap. A dark object rose in front of us. The plane stopped with a splintering crash, and I was flung headlong from my seat.

CHAPTER XVI

WHEN I began to take vague notice of my surroundings, my head was lying upon something soft. Everything was dark above me. I stretched out a hand and touched wet earth. I lay still, trying to understand, but my brain was dull and numbed. I tried to sit up.

A hand pressed me down. I puzzled over that; a thought entered my brain like a shock. Vinton had me! I was a prisoner!

With a hoarse cry I struggled to free myself. The restraining hand pressed me back.

"Wait a little," said a gentle, low-toned voice.

"Mary!" I gasped.

"Yes, it's Mary. Keep quiet, please—just for a little while."

I sighed contentedly and my head fell back in her lap. Presently I started violently.

"Vinton!" I exclaimed. "Where's Vinton?"

"Miles and miles away," she said soothingly. "Don't you remember?"

Her cool hand was on my forehead, and I lay still, with a luxurious feeling of languor.

"What's my name?" I asked complacently.

"Mansfield—Daniel Mansfield," she answered. "The aëroplane—you remember that?"

She must be referring to somebody else when she spoke of Daniel Mansfield. But at the mention of the airplane memory surged over me. I struggled to a sitting posture.

"You're not hurt?" I exclaimed.

"I don't seem to be," she answered. "I've been sitting here at least ten minutes."

"It knocked me out, I guess—that landing," I said, a little ashamed I had proved the weaker, yet overjoyed to find that Mary had come out of the accident unharmed. "We hit something, didn't we?"

"A snake fence," she replied. "I stopped with the machine, but you went over the fence."

"Where are we?"

"Sitting in the middle of a road just now—where you landed. I climbed over the fence and found you. I—I thought you were dead, at first."

There was a catch in her voice.

"I'm a long way from dead," I assured her, reaching out and stroking one of her hands. "It was good of you, Mary. I'm going to see what it feels like to stand up."

I rose shakily to my feet, swayed a bit, then got a grip on myself. My legs, aside from the wrenched ankle that was not so painful as it had been, seemed to be all right, but there was a dull ache in my side, and I was dizzy. Mary sat in the road, looking up at me in the dim light. The fog through which we had descended hung low on the earth.

"Is—is there anything the matter with your arm—your left arm?" she inquired suddenly, rising from her place and stepping close to me.

I looked down at the arm in question, and saw it was hanging in a curiously limp fashion at my side. Cautiously I felt of it.

"It's broken—above the elbow," I said, after an examination. "But it doesn't hurt. I can't feel it at all."

She uttered a quick exclamation of anxiety.

"We must get help right away," she declared. "You'll need a doctor."

"But how about you?" I asked anxiously.

"It's curious, but I seem to be all right, except for a shaking up." She stretched her arms above her head, moved them slowly down to her sides, then stepped two or three paces away from me and back. "Yes; I think I'm all right," she added judicially. "But you're not. Come—if you think you can walk."

"Come where?"

"Anywhere—along the road, I suppose," she answered. "We can't stay here."

"I want to have a look at the machine first," I told her. "Which way is it?"

"Over there," she answered, pointing behind me. "But you're not fit to do anything. Don't bother with it."

I stumbled across the road until I came to a heap of wreckage. In the darkness I could not tell which was machine and which was fence, so inextricably were they entangled. I surveyed the litter, turned back to Mary and said:

"Let's go, then. Which way?"

"I don't know that it makes any difference," she answered; "but in one direction it seems to be down-hill. That ought to be easier."

"We'll try it down-hill for a while, then," I agreed.

I linked my good arm in one of hers, and together we started slowly down the road. It was a fairly good country thoroughfare; so good, in fact, that I felt we could not be at any great distance from dwellings. The fog was dense, and the night air decidedly sharp. I could feel Mary, in her thin blue dress, shivering.

"Take my coat," I said, stopping and beginning to remove it.

She protested earnestly, saying I must not allow my broken arm to become chilled; but I would not listen, and finally forced her to place the garment across her shoulders. We went along slowly, descending a gentle slope in the road until we reached a stretch of level going. Now and then we came to turns, but there was no sign of life anywhere. Once or twice we stopped and listened, but could hear nothing.

"It can't be very far to somewhere," I said reassuringly.

"I'm sure it can't," she answered. "Does your arm hurt badly?"

It had not yet begun to pain me, being still numb with the shock that had broken it. As it swung loosely at my side, I could not feel that there was any arm there at all.

"Feel in my hip pocket and see if there are any matches there, will you? It's the only pocket I didn't try in the plane. And if you can find any, will you reach into my side coat pocket and get me a cigarette?" I asked.

She reached into my hip pocket and triumphantly held up the remainder of a card of matches. She fumbled in my coat pocket, found the cigarette I asked for, and laughed curiously.

"There's something else in there," she remarked. "The dictaphone cylinder I used for a weight in the chimney."

"I must have stuck it in my pocket; I don't know why," I explained. "Is it broken?"

"It doesn't seem to be," she replied, as she took two cigarettes out of the box and struck a match. "Think I'll have one, too."

The tiny light flamed redly, and we both burst out laughing. Mary's usually well-kept hair was tossed in wild abandon, her face was mottled with smears of chimney soot, her dress was grimed and torn. My own appearance must have matched hers to perfection.

"A pair of scarecrows!" I exclaimed. "The fog didn't wash off much of the make-up."

"You have a cut on your forehead," she said, with sudden seriousness. "Let me tie it up. Have you a handkerchief?"

I found one and bent my head down to her, while she fashioned a bandage out of it.

"We're lucky people," I observed, as we started along the road arm in arm. "What did you think as we dived down into that fog?"

"What did you think?" she parried.

"I thought it was good-by," I answered frankly.

"So did I," she agreed in a low voice. "But it was better—far better—than—"

Her voice broke off and I could feel her tremble.

"We'll not become reminiscent," I said abruptly. "Not so recently reminiscent, anyhow. I think we had better talk about other things."

"For instance?"

"Oh, anything—Balboa."

I heard her laugh softly.

"Do you remember the date?" she asked.

"No; do you?"

"September 25, 1513."

"I can't dispute it," I said. "I'm hazy; but I've still got that dime I won."

"Really? The same dime?"

"It's in a special pocket. I'm never going to spend it. It's a nucleus."

"A nucleus? For what?"

"Who knows?" I answered, tightening my grip on her arm.

"I'm sure I don't," she said.

Such talk, of course, was all by way of trying to deceive ourselves; it did not interpret what was really in our minds. It was just trivial bravado, to show each other we were light-hearted and unconcerned over our mishaps; although I knew full well it was too shallow to mislead either of us.

Even in the face of death, people will joke. We were in no such strait as that, yet there was the same unreality in the things we were saying to each other. That Mary and I both understood the situation there was not the least doubt. In our hearts we were serious and thoughtful; but our lips were framing light phrases, each trying to sustain the courage of the other in make-believe fashion.

"I think we've made some sort of record for some kind of night flight that has never been tried before," I said, as we plodded on slowly in the darkness.

"I should hope so," she answered earnestly. "But, oh, Mr. Mansfield, wasn't it glorious up there among the stars?"

"Glorious? Perhaps—while we stayed up—Mary!"

"And so exciting when we came down—Mr. Mansfield!"

"And thrilling when we hit—Mary!"

I could hear her laughing as she looked up at me. "But, Mr. Mansfield—"

"See here," I interrupted, "we're at cross-purposes. We don't seem to be working on the same job. Now, you're either Miss Donaldson or you're Mary; I'm either Mr. Mansfield or I'm Dan. Somehow, I got the idea you were Mary. If you're Mary, then I'm not Mr. Mansfield. Now who *are* you?"

"Why, I guess I'm Mary," she said. "I seem to have been—for some time."

"Then who am I?"

"Daniel Vasco Nuñez Balboa Mansfield," she repeated glibly.

"Which, in short form, is—"

"Dan, I suppose," she said meekly.

"You shouldn't be so stubborn about some things," I grumbled. "You've called me so many names, you know."

"Now who's reminiscing?"

"I'm guilty," I answered contritely. "I forgot. Everything's present and future from now on."

It was just more of the same sort of talk, all for the purpose of making light of our troubles.

Yet, when we had walked for what seemed an age along that aimless, fog-bound road, without passing a single human being, or even a light by the wayside, or hearing a sound that would guide us to fellow beings, I began to think we should soon tire of jesting. Mary was shivering from the cold, and I could tell from the reluctance of her footsteps that she was getting weary. My arm was beginning to awaken to sensations. A dull pain above the elbow, extending to the shoulder, warned me the stunned nerves were rousing themselves, and that I might soon expect real suffering unless I had prompt attention.

I never traveled a road that seemed to lead nowhere so persistently. There was little of which to complain in the grades, for most of them were too gentle to be of account, even to the weary; but it turned and twisted in an exasperating manner, as if it had no purpose or destination. Everything about us was silent, while the fog-shroud hung close and dense.

Once we sat down on a large boulder at the roadside to rest, but it was too chilly to long remain inactive.

"I feel sleepy," she confided, as we resumed our journey.

"I'm hungry," I added. "And thirsty. And in a hurry to get somewhere."

"Your arm!" she cried, with quick intuition. "Has it begun to pain—Dan?"

"I didn't mean that," I answered untruthfully. "But I'm afraid you're getting tired, Mary."

"I'll try to walk faster—if you think your ankle will let you," she said stoutly, quickening her pace; but I could feel it cost her an effort.

We came to a forking of roads.

"Which way?" I asked uncertainly.

"Listen!" she commanded.

We stood silent, and, faintly, there came a sound of music. It seemed ever so far away; the thought of walking to it repelled me.

"It's over that way," she said, pointing to the right.

"Then we'll take the right fork," I answered. "Come on!"

We stumbled along the new pathway, and soon something tall and dark and colossal loomed on either side of the road.

"Looks like a private gateway," I muttered. "We must be getting somewhere."

We passed the portals, and the road, because of in-terlocked branches of trees overhead, became almost invisible in the fog and darkness. Two or three times we strayed from it, finding ourselves on heavy, damp grass. The sounds of music became more distinct.

"It's somebody's estate," said Mary, clinging to my arm and dragging her feet slowly. "Suppose there are dogs!"

"I'll hug them!" I answered. "Dogs, men or any-thing. Let's find somebody."

There was nothing visible as we staggered onward. Mary grew more limp at every step; although she had sustained no real injury from our abrupt descent the shock was beginning to assert itself in reaction. I slipped my right arm about her waist and hobbled along, half carrying her. The ache in my side seemed to have disappeared, but my broken arm was throbbing, and its every movement was translated into acute pain.

The music ceased, and in its stead came a sound of laughter, as if many voices were blended in the mirth.

"It can't be far," I said to her. "Keep up a little longer."

"I will," she answered bravely, but her figure sagged against me as she spoke.

"A light!" I cried. "See it?"

She nodded wearily, without speaking, and scarcely looking up.

It did not seem like a single light, but filtered through

the fog in a glow. The laughter was distinct; there was a babel of voices. The road we traveled curved sharply toward the glow.

Under a great porte-cochère we paused, looking up at a snow-white mansion. Floods of yellow light streamed from its windows; the great doors in front were thrown wide; there was a radiation of warmth and high spirits from within. And still the chorus of laughter was uplifted.

"It's—it's almost like the White House!" I exclaimed stupidly.

"It can't be," she answered, leaning heavily against me. "But even if it was?"

"We'll go in," I declared, tightening my grip on her and half lifting her up the steps that led to a broad porch.

As we approached the open doors, a grotesque figure darted out and almost ran into us. We drew back with an involuntary start. The thing was a circus clown— chalked face, fool's cap, Elizabethan ruff, absurdly loose jacket and pantaloons. Crescents were painted upon his cheeks; there was a ridiculous black dot on the end of his nose.

He stared at us, then wheeled with a shout, and bounded back into the brightly lighted hall.

"Here at last!" I heard him cry at the top of a shrill voice. "The pair of them. And, oh, what sights!"

Mary and I crossed the threshold and entered the house. There was a smooth, waxed floor under our feet, and I remember recovering my balance with difficulty as I slipped. The next moment we were surrounded by a crowding mob of extraordinary-looking beings.

A woman in the crowd cried:

"Perfect! Perfect! But what are they?"

In front of us stood an aged man in a long, flowing robe, with a scythe in his hand and an amazingly large hour-glass stuck under his arm. To his left was the most disreputable tramp I ever laid eyes upon, with reddened eyes, a dirty slouch hat upon his head, and a tin can dangling from a string he held in his hand.

Next was a dainty little yellow-haired girl, who looked like *Columbine*. Back in the ranks I could see a devil, dressed all in red, with a sinister goatee and mustache. At the right of the old man with the scythe stood a shepherdess; then a gorgeous brunette with a tambourine and a brilliant red and yellow gown that came far above her knees; a stately lady with powdered hair and a couple of black patches upon her cheek. Mixed in a mad confusion, were soldiers, and admirals, and milkmaids, and ambassadors, and Indian princes, and ballet girls, and monks, and bathing beauties— every incongruous being that might be grouped together from the ends of the earth.

"Must we guess?" called a voice.

"What a wonderful get-up!" I heard somebody whisper.

The hall in which we stood was of the old colonial type. A wide staircase ascended in the middle of it.

From either side of it extended great rooms that were a blaze of light.

I stared at the array of figures in front of me, and down at Mary. My arm was around her, and she was shrinking close to me, one hand clutching at my sleeve. Her eyes were wide with wonder.

"Such a pose!" cried the tramp, banging his tin can noisily on the floor. "Great! Great!"

"In with them!" shouted a turbaned prince.

The motley crowd closed upon us, and we were carried along like chips on a swiftly flowing tide. Somebody grabbed my broken arm roughly, and I cried out with pain, but none heeded me. On into a big room we were swept, across its glossy floor, and upon a dais canopied with flowers. The crowd fell away from us.

"Announce yourselves!" cried a red-coated soldier in stentorian tones.

All I could do was to look down at Mary, who was clinging to me, her face half hidden against my shirt.

"Announce! Announce!" came a chorus. "You must announce!"

My eyes roved over the crowd, but my throat seemed paralyzed.

"It's the rule," said the old man with the scythe, waving it at me. "Everybody has announced. Tell us what you are."

"For Heaven's sake, what are we—where are we?" I whispered to Mary, bending my head toward her.

"Shipwrecked couple!" suggested a show girl, in a

little blue and white. "A hero and his fair bride, just off a desert isle!"

"Nonsense!" retorted an admiral. "The hero isn't barefooted."

"The downtrod! The Poverty Hollow delegation!" proclaimed a cowled monk. "Give poverty a great big hand!"

"Railroad wreck!"

"Bargain-day victims!"

"Explosion!"

"Subway sardines!"

"Adam and Eve kicked out of a modern Eden!"

"Joy-riders!"

The din was bewildering. The red devil and the brunette with the tambourine started a wild dance in an open space in front of the dais. A king's fool shook his bells under our noses and grimaced. Off at the other end of the room the music started playing.

"I knew the Forshews were planning some stunt—but what are they?" whispered a voice close to me.

"That isn't Billy Forshew."

"Sure it is; it must be! He's just blacked up."

"But look at his wife! She's a sight!"

A girl, slender and delicate, edged her way through the crowd and stood staring up at us from under a big Gainsborough hat. She turned and whispered something to a young man at her elbow, and both stared at us fixedly. He stepped close to us.

"This *is* Forshew, isn't it?" he asked politely.

"It is *not!*" I answered, at last finding my voice.

A hush came over the crowd, the music stopped, and the devil and the dancing girl came to a pause.

"Who are you, then?" he asked in a puzzled tone.

"My name is Mansfield."

"Mansfield?" He did not seem to understand.

"Certainly; Mansfield. And this—"

"I don't quite understand yet," he continued politely. "We expected a Mr. and Mrs. Forshew."

"We're just two people looking for some help," I blurted angrily.

"Help! Help! They're looking for Help!" cried the king's fool. "Where's Help? Fetch out Help! Who's playing Help?"

The young man who stood before us silenced him with a gesture.

"We've had an accident," I went on impatiently. "This lady is exhausted."

"An accident?"

"An airplane accident."

The young man fell back a pace and regarded me with incredulous eyes. I could feel Mary leaning against me heavily.

My interlocutor turned to the girl in the Gainsborough hat and whispered to her. She seemed bewildered.

"An aviator from Mars! A Martian and a Martianette!" cackled a gray-whiskered ambassador.

A tall, elderly gentleman of distinguished appearance, attired in conventional evening dress, pushed his way through the crowd. The girl in the Gainsborough hat turned to him and said something.

"For heaven's sake," I cried, advancing down the two steps that led to the main floor, half carrying Mary in my arm, "don't mistake this for any masquerade! This lady and I have had an accident. We wandered in here, expecting to find somebody who might help us. If we can't get assistance here, will you kindly tell us where to go?"

The old gentleman raised his hand imperatively, and the crowd became silent. Mary swayed against me and began to slip from my grasp. My arm was aching horribly.

The Gainsborough girl ran forward, put her arms about the helpless figure, and supported Mary with surprising strength. A monk seized her in his arms and lifted her as if she were a child. The young man who had interrogated me and one of the Oriental princes grabbed me on either side, for I had begun to stagger drunkenly.

"Upstairs, at once!" commanded the old gentleman quietly. "Fetch some brandy, Harry. Here is what good pre-war stuff is for. Call Dr. Graham; he's somewhere about. Don't crowd around, please!"

He made a passage through the staring throng of masqueraders, and we went out of the big room.

CHAPTER XVII

THE room in which I lay, blinking at the morning sunlight, was the pleasantest place imaginable. There was nothing cramped or ungenerous about it. The windows were wide and high; the four-poster in which I lay was gigantic. Everything was white and clean and restful. I felt strangely comfortable.

They had taken me to that room the night before, the Oriental prince and the young man who could not understand, and between them had managed to undress me and put me to bed. It was the prince who discovered I had a broken arm. They told me Dr. Graham would be in presently. It may have been Dr. Graham who came in, but he was dressed like a *Pinafore* sailor. None the less, he had a surgical kit with him.

"How's Mary?" I had demanded of him even before he was introduced.

"The young lady? Oh, she's going to be all right after a good rest. Just shaken up. Let's see the arm."

"You're sure about her?"

"Sure. Hello! A nice simple fracture. Hurts, does it? We'll shoot a little dope into it first," he said easily. "Ho, you princeling! Bring a flock of hot water here."

I was getting drowsy before he had finished with the splints, but I still had Mary in my mind.

"Go back to her at once!" I commanded.

"All right," said the man in the sailor clothes, with a laugh.

"Tell her I'm all right."

"Oh, she knows that. I've already sent word to her. Hold still with that arm a minute!"

"Tell her I asked," I went on sleepily. "And then come back and—"

"Say, do you think all I've got to do is to run back and forth from one room to the other, telling each of you that the other is all right? She's asked me ten times already, and I've told her." The doctor was grinning cheerfully. "Told her nine times before I even looked at you. She seems to have a mania for reiterated information."

I smiled foolishly and tried to keep my eyes open.

"Thinks you're some wonder, too," he added, as he applied the finishing touches to my arm. "Keeps on telling me that airplane yarn. I suppose you want to tell it, too. Don't! It'll land you in the nut college if you keep on repeating it. Truth, now, that airplane was a motor car, wasn't it?"

"No, it wasn't," I answered resentfully. "Go and see for yourself. And tell Mary—"

"I'm going to tell all the rest of it to Sweeney," said the doctor, as he pulled the covers up over me. "You for the hay, now. And if that stuff I gave you doesn't put you to sleep, I'm coming in to chloroform you. Good-night!"

"But don't forget to tell—"

I heard him laugh as he went out the door, his ridiculous sailor trousers flapping about his ankles. I think I must have fallen asleep instantly.

As I lay there the next morning looking at the sunlight that streaked in through the flowered curtains, it seemed as if all of it must have been a dream. Only when I attempted to move my arm, and it ached dully, did I completely awaken to the fact that there had been no nightmare, that all the confused maze of images in my mind represented events.

I had been awake perhaps a quarter of an hour when the man who had set my arm entered the room. He was no longer a comic opera jacky. He looked like a regular doctor—a fairly young one, too.

"How goes it?" he asked, shaking hands.

"How's Mary?"

"Grand!" he answered, laughing. "She's been down to breakfast. It's ten o'clock."

"Why can't I go down?" I demanded, sitting up.

He sent me back on the pillow with a push.

"Because you're busted up and Mary isn't," he answered. "Maybe I'll let you go down after a while. Arm hurt?"

"No. Did you tell her—"

He shoved a thermometer into my mouth and laughed at me.

"Say!" he exclaimed suddenly. "They found the airplane all right! Sent some men down the road at daylight. I thought sure you were having a hop dream last night." He removed the thermometer and examined it. "You're not playing according to Hoyle," he remarked. "No fever. You're not enough trouble to be interesting. But Lord, man! You must have had a crazy night."

"Did Mary tell you?"

"She's told about all of it, I guess, by this time. She certainly does recommend you, son. Engaged, I suppose?"

He asked it with good-natured, breezy impudence.

"No," I answered. "But say, doctor—"

"Not engaged, eh? Chance for me, then. Believe me, my friend, Mary is *some* girl!"

I sat up with sudden energy.

"Now, you look here!" I said sharply. "That young lady—"

"Is going to be engaged. All right, old man; what you say goes. My chance disappears. I weep; I repine; I congratulate you. Now, let me tell you something about that arm. It's not bad enough to make a hero out of you. It's scientifically simple. It'll be all right and as straight as a string after the bone knits. You can get up some time to-day, if you behave yourself and stay on the ground and cut out the aviation for a while. Are you willing to take orders?"

"No trouble about the flying," I answered. "I'm

off that for good. But, for Heaven's sake, what did we break in on, last night?"

"Oh, just a little house-party. I suppose it dazzled you. Too bad it took us so long to wake up! We all thought you were the Billy Forshews. As a matter of fact, they never showed up at all; missed their train."

"Where are we?" I demanded.

The door opened softly and Mary stepped into the room.

"She'll tell you," said the doctor, rising from my bedside and smiling indulgently. "I'll be back to have another look at you this afternoon."

He walked out, with a friendly grin at Mary, and left us alone.

She paused half-way across the room, looking at me with apprehension in her eyes; then she came over to the bed quickly and bent over me.

"Hello, Mary!" I said, reaching out a hand to her.

"You're all right?" she asked anxiously.

"Fine as a fiddle," I answered, smiling.

"I was worried," she went on gravely. "But they wouldn't allow you to be disturbed. Does your arm pain you very much?"

I shook my head as I looked up at her. She was fair and sweet, and a sunbeam that stole through the window made her dark hair shine like satin. Her cheeks were pale and there was an anxious look about her eyes, but she looked well, none the less. Her tall, slender figure was gowned in a simple white linen dress that made her look like the lily of the garden-party, save for the shortness of the skirt which barely reached her knee-caps, an inch or so shorter than Mary wore her own dresses. In it she seemed like a little girl. She flushed faintly as she saw me studying her.

"Doesn't hurt at all," I answered, after a pause. "Please tell me where we are—if you know."

"We're in West Virginia," she answered, seating herself at the side of the bed.

"From the way we were going, I thought we must be close to the Mississippi, at least," I commented.

"No; West Virginia," she went on. "They've been down to see the airplane; it's hopelessly wrecked, they say. One of the men brought back your compass. That's all smashed, too. It's a pity!"

"I can build another," I said carelessly. "But go on."

"It was a masquerade we came to," she continued. "There's a big house-party here; lots of young people. They're out riding to the hounds this morning. They couldn't believe, at first, we were not part of the masquerade."

"I thought they'd never wake up," I grumbled.

"Oh, but they're lovely!" she exclaimed. "This is Major Nesbit's house; he's some big man in this part of the state, I understand. The Nesbits are entertaining about twenty young people here, and last night there were a lot of the neighbors, too. They're doing everything in the world for us. Do you remember the little girl in the Gainsborough hat?"

I nodded.

"She's the daughter. She's adorable. I'm—I'm wearing one of her dresses."

"So I see," I answered, glancing at the hem of the gown.

Mary gave an ineffectual tug toward pulling the scant skirt over her knees and went on:

"Dr. Graham lives near here. He's been awfully kind—everybody has. They're so interested in what happened to us. They wouldn't believe a lot of it until they found the plane."

"Have you told them everything?"

"Not—everything," she answered slowly; "but a good deal. They think it's romantic."

"Well, is it?" I asked bluntly.

"I don't know. I suppose it depends on the point of view. Major Nesbit is a dear, and so is Mrs. Nesbit. They want us to stay just as long as we will. The party has just begun. But, of course, you can't stay—with that arm."

"Oh, I don't know," I answered, trying to move it.

From what I could see, it looked like a pretty nice place in which to stay. It was restful; it was home-like.

"It seems queer to be uninvited guests among strangers," she added. "But they really seem to want us, Dan."

I liked to hear her call me Dan; I lay quiet and closed my eyes, letting the word sink in.

"And, while I can," she said, her voice sinking low,

"I want to thank you for all you have done for me; to thank you from the bottom of my heart."

"I don't see what you have to thank me for," I answered, opening my eyes and reaching for her hands. "What's been accomplished?"

"I've—I've escaped from the spell," she whispered. "It's all past now!"

I found one of her hands and held it.

"Then it has indeed been worth while," I told her.

Momentarily she let me keep her cool, slender fingers; then, with a sudden contraction of her forehead and a sharp intake of her breath, she drew her hand away and began staring out of the sunlit window. It was as if some recollection had flashed over her. I lay there smiling. There was something I knew, and Mary didn't.

A knock on the door, and Major Nesbit entered the room.

"Good morning and congratulations," he said, as he crossed over to the bed. "Dr. Graham tells me there is nothing serious. I am glad, sir—very glad! And I wish to apologize for myself, my family, and my guests. We were slow to understand last night—unpardonably slow. I fear we caused you unnecessary pain. Miss Donaldson"—he turned to her with a courtly bow— "has told us much of your adventure, Mr. Mansfield. It is extraordinary—extraordinary. It is the desire of Mrs. Nesbit and myself that you should remain with us as long as you will. We should be charmed if you could remain with us until you are completely recovered, sir.

We wish to add you and Miss Donaldson to our house-party. We shall try to make it congenial. The house is yours; our hospitality is yours. My daughter is already in love with your *fiancée*, sir. We feel honored to have you both."

I did not dare look at Mary, but in a confused way I tried to thank the old gentleman who stood at my bed-side. Why was it that all these people assumed Mary to be my *fiancée?*

After a further urging of his cordial invitation to remain his guests, Major Nesbit withdrew, and Mary escaped with him. I tried to detain her. She affected not to understand, but I could not fail to note the high color in her cheeks as she followed him out of the room.

They left me alone for a while. I occupied the time trying to summarize events and put them in their relation to one another. What was the result of it all?

First, I had been mysteriously shadowed at the behest of a tall man. I had passed under an *alias* at the White House. I had committed an apparent robbery of a messenger-boy. I had forced my way into a strange house and explored it like a burglar. I had played the bandit in a prominent hotel. I had lost the hand of a girl who had promised to be my wife. I had been made a prisoner. I had turned myself into a chimney-sweep. I had recovered a stolen paper and had, in turn, been despoiled of it. I had stolen an airplane and wrecked it. I had destroyed the only existing model of a device upon which I had spent more than a year of labor. I had—

It made me dizzy to think of what I had done. And the business was not yet two days old! A fine record of achievement for a man who had always believed himself a law-abiding citizen!

What had been gained?

I was puzzling over it when I fell asleep, and I did not waken until a maid brought a tray into my room. She was followed by the young man who, with the Indian potentate, had half carried me up the stairs the night before.

"My name is Harvey Nesbit," he said, extending his hand. "Awfully sorry we bothered you so much last night, but we didn't understand. Dr. Graham says after you've had your lunch you can come downstairs, if you want to. I'm to help you dress."

I liked young Nesbit. We talked while I devoured the lunch on the tray, and then he helped me get into a suit of his clothes. We were of about the same size and build, and I did not look unpresentable, save for the sling which held my arm.

It was a dazzling spring afternoon as I walked out on the broad porch with him. A dozen or so young men and girls in riding togs were there, talking and laughing; but there was a sudden hush as I appeared. It was plain I was an object of intense curiosity. Gradually they began to crowd about me until young Nesbit waved them away good-naturedly.

"Give him a chance," he laughed. "No doubt Mr.

Mansfield will tell us all about it when he is ready."

He steered me around a corner of the porch to a shaded place where I saw Mary, sitting with the girl of the Gainsborough and an elderly sweet-faced woman whom I guessed to be Major Nesbit's wife. I was introduced to my hostesses who, after a few minutes, withdrew and left Mary alone with me.

Mary was demure as I seated myself near her in one of the big wicker chairs. Both of us, I think, had a feeling of constraint. Two or three minutes of silence ensued.

"Well, Mary?" I said at length, studying her serious face.

"Well—what?"

She laughed in an embarrassed way.

"We seem to have a breathing-spell," I wound up lamely.

"Isn't it lovely here? I wish we *could* stay."

"Why not? They seem to want us. I think both of us could stand a little rest."

"But I shall have to go back."

"Back to where?"

She shrugged her shoulders.

"I don't know that I'm in any hurry to go back," I said.

She looked at me inquiringly.

"You see, I've committed larceny in both Washington and Baltimore," I explained. "It may be healthier for me to stay away for a while."

"I'm sorry," she murmured. "I've caused you a lot of trouble, haven't I—Dan?"

"We've been some trouble to each other," I admitted, searching her eyes until she colored. "I think we've become responsible for each other, in a way."

"Responsible?"

"Yes. You began it, which makes you responsible. I refused to quit, which makes me responsible. And, do you know, I rather like the responsibility!"

She favored me with a quick glance, then directed her gaze out across the great lawn.

"They all seem to think we're engaged," I added irrelevantly.

Mary made no answer.

"And why can't we be?" I asked abruptly.

She gave me a swift look of astonishment, and buried her face in her hands.

"Don't! Don't!" she exclaimed, shrinking from me.

"I know we haven't known each other very long," I said, leaning forward. "It's scarcely forty-eight hours. But I know this—I love you, Mary!"

"Please!" Her voice was agitated.

"But why shouldn't I tell you? Just because of short acquaintance? That's a reason that counts little with me."

"Can't you see?" she cried, raising her eyes to mine. "Don't you undersand? Have you forgotten the—the girl—"

I laughed quietly, while she stared at me in amazement.

"That was ended yesterday morning," I said. "It seems as if it had never existed. Now it's over, I can't understand how it ever happened. I loved you before it was over."

"It is ended?" she repeated slowly.

"Absolutely. She even gave me back the ring."

"The ring?"

"And I gave it to a little girl on the street who said her name was not Fanny," I added.

I believe she thought I was light-headed; she did not speak. At last she ventured:

"Was it because of what happened at the White House?"

"That was the cause, Mary. Wasn't it lucky? It gave me the right to love you. Do you think, dear, you can care enough for me to—"

She had risen from her chair and stood before me, straight and proud, her dark eyes tender and shining.

"I think," she said falteringly, "that if I have deprived you of anything, Dan, it is only fair to make restitution. That is—"

"Mary!" I cried, starting to my feet and reaching for her.

"Beg pardon," said a voice behind me. "Hope I'm not intruding; but I must tell you of this."

With a gesture of annoyance, I fear, I turned and confronted young Nesbit. He was smiling at us, and in his hand he held toward me a dictaphone cylinder.

"I'm afraid I've done something pretty rude," he went on. "We had to have your clothes cleaned up,

Mr. Mansfield, and in taking things out of the pockets I found this. Dad has one of those machines in the house. He uses it, and I do some of my law work here. I was so curious about the affair I took the liberty of slipping it into my machine. I suppose you know what the cylinder is?"

Mary and I looked at each other and back at the cylinder.

"No," I said; "I've no idea."

"Come into the library a moment," he suggested, leading the way.

We followed him wonderingly, and watched him slip the cylinder into place on a dictaphone that stood at the side of the big table. There was a double set of earpieces, and he handed Mary and me one each.

"No, listen," he said, as he placed them to our ears.

He turned a switch and the cylinder began to revolve. There was a confused buzzing, and then I heard:

I, Rufus Jennings, being of sound and disposing mind and memory, do hereby declare this to be my last will and testament, expressly revoking all other wills and testaments made by me prior to the one I now execute.

I direct that after my lawful and just debts shall have been paid—

Mary dropped the receiver with a little cry.

"It's Uncle Rufus!" she exclaimed, her cheeks pale.

"The missing will!" I cried. "You recognize his voice?"

"Perfectly!"

The cylinder went on, and the dictaphone repeated into my ears the clear, rather sharp voice of Rufus Jennings. Mary listened, too.

We heard it to the end. In some respects it did not differ materially from the will Vinton had in his possession, although it bequeathed to Mary more than one-fifth of the property, and made no provision for an income to be settled upon her husband. The date of it, as declared in the voice of Jennings himself, was recent—clearly later than the written document I had gained and lost.

Mary and I looked at each other stupefied as the last words on the cylinder were repeated. The chimney weight—the thing I had absent-mindedly thrust into my pocket, and which had by pure luck escaped destruction when the airplane crashed to earth—was the last will of Rufus Jennings!

"Are you a lawyer?" I demanded of young Nesbit.

"I practice at law," he admitted, smiling.

"Can you tell me if a will like that is legal?"

"It beats me," he answered, knitting his forehead. "It would probably depend on circumstances. If there were witnesses, for instance—"

"It can be proved he spoke of this will," I said, excitedly, remembering the butler, Howard, to whom Uncle Rufus had spoken just before he died.

"That might help," said Nesbit. "There are cases where verbal wills have been probated. This seems to be neither a verbal nor a written will. I never heard of such a case."

"But if it could be shown it was this testator's habit to leave his records upon dictaphone cylinders?"

"That might help, too," he admitted. "Particularly if the will did not happen to be contested. In a contest, of course, with a written will against it—why—well, to tell you the truth, I don't believe there's a precedent for such a situation. If you'll excuse me, I'm going to dig for a while among my books. It's an extraordinary case—extraordinary!"

As young Nesbit left the room, I turned to Mary and cried exultantly:

"You can fight Vinton now! He doesn't hold the last will!"

She nodded mechanically and began playing with a paper-cutter on the table.

"Don't you see?" I went on excitedly. "Here's a weapon—"

I stopped short. Mary was not the least interested. Presently she looked up at me, accusation in her eyes.

"Why, Mary!" I exclaimed. "What is it?"

"I wasn't thinking about the will," she said waveringly. "I don't care about it. Only I was thinking if you really meant what you said—"

I sprang toward her, but stopped short as the figure of Major Nesbit entered the library.

"The papers have just come up from town," he said. "I thought you might care to look at them."

I took them from him with rather bad grace, exasperated at the new interruption. Mary played with her paper-cutter. Her cheeks were flushed.

I was mechanically glancing at the first page of one of the papers, when my eye fell upon a Baltimore date line. Major Nesbit slipped out of the room while I was reading it. It read:

A man believed, from papers found upon his person, to have been Robert Vinton was found dead last night on the rear lawn of the estate of the late Rufus Jennings, near this city. There was a bullet wound in the dead man's head and a heavy service revolver lay on the ground near the body. In his hand was a small automatic. The nearest neighbors to the Jennings estate are at some distance, but they reported to the State Police who were called by an untraced phone message that they had heard what they believed to have been a number of shots, fired in rapid succession, early in the evening. There was nobody on the estate when the police arrived. An investigation to determine whether Vinton died by his own hand or was murdered is under way.

Vinton was dead! In a flash I believed I knew the explanation. Vinton, leaping from the hurriedly returning limousine, and first in pursuit, had intercepted a bullet fired by either Lazare or Purvis at the escaping plane. His companions had fled—and the police had Vinton's papers—including the will!

"Vinton will never trouble you, Mary," I said, trying to steady my voice, as I handed her the paper.

She read the account slowly, bowed her head and stood motionless. I paced the room, watching her, not wishing to disturb her reflections. At last she raised her eyes and looked at me.

"It makes no difference about the wills—now," I said. She smiled at me faintly and walked over toward one of the windows, where she stood in the sunlight. I was too much astonished by the strange succession of events to make a move until she turned her head and gazed at me, a wistful look in her eyes. I strode across the library.

"I can't find a single precedent," said the voice of young Nesbit behind me. "It's a wonderful case!"

I turned upon him with a beseeching look and made a gesture. He comprehended, nodded at me, and stepped quickly out of the room, closing the door after him.

"Now, Mary!" I said, putting my arm about her and drawing her close.

"I—I thought it was about time," she whispered, her face against my shoulder, her young, white arms about my neck.

THE END

www.ingramcontent.com/pod-product-compliance
Lightning Source LLC
Chambersburg PA
CBHW020817260626
47169CB00003B/700